The ADVENT

A catalogue record for this book is available from the National Library of Australia

www.brotherbrad.com

The Advent

The Birth of Jesus Christ

BROTHER BRAD SMITH

Dedication

All praise to the God and Father
of our Lord Jesus Christ.

Dear reader, I pray that this publication will help
you to deepen your relationship with Jesus.

Acknowledgements

There are many people who have inspired and encouraged me over the years to write, and to continue writing. My wife Elissa has missed my presence in early mornings, late evenings and weekends when I set aside time to read through numerous historical and Biblical documents, stories and archives to be able to formulate a proper and reasonable account of the events that lead up to Christmas, and has been cheering me on. I am grateful for her encouragement.

Initially I turned to Daniel Darling's book *The Characters of Christmas* to gain fresh insight into how we may encounter various members of the Christmas story. This helped me gain the historical perspective of Elizabeth and Zechariah, the shepherds and Herod.

I found encouragement when reading Scot McKnight's *The Real Mary* which presents a balanced view for the character of Mary (Jesus' mother), which helped me shape her character in various chapters of this book.

References to the purposes of the stars and how the magi may have interpreted them can be primarily attributed to reading Marilyn Hickey's, *Signs in the Heavens*.

I also relied on research from my first publication *Via Crucis Via Lucis: The Way of the Cross The Way of the Light* to continue the flow of the storyline between the events of Easter and Christmas in this publication.

Special thanks to my friendly beta readers who provided feedback and comments to make the quality of this book grammatically better than the first draft and improve the readability: Ray Woodrow (author), Ps Sally Davis and Gary Weston (former missionary to Japan).

There were also a variety of online information sources that provided food for thought and debate, which were considered in the writing and presentation of this publication, though I can't name them all here. Two of the more relevant ones are listed below.

Contents

	Introduction	13
Advent 1:	The Curse	17
Advent 2:	The Priest	29
Advent 3:	The Covenant	37
Advent 4:	The Blessing	45
Advent 5:	The Dream	53
Advent 6:	The Sceptre	61
Advent 7:	The Ruler	71
Advent 8:	The Shoot	83
Advent 9:	The Builder	97
Advent 10:	The Virgin	107
Advent 11:	The Angel Gabriel	117
Advent 12:	The Unbelieving Priest	127
Advent 13:	The Lord's Servant	139
Advent 14:	The Pregnant Cousin	151

Advent 15: The Righteous Man 163

Advent 16: The Innkeeper 179

Advent 17: The Little Town 187

Advent 18: The Stall 195

Advent 19: The Shepherds 203

Advent 20: The Star 211

Advent 21: The King 221

Advent 22: The Glory of Israel 229

Advent 23: The Prophetess 237

Advent 24: The Plan 243

Concluding Thoughts 255

About the Author 257

Other Books by Brother Brad Smith 259

Introduction

It was one week after the publication of Via *Crucis Via Lucis: The Way of the Cross The Way of the Light* and I was feeling pretty good that I managed to publish my first book as a work of contemporary Christian literature for the Easter period. That was October 2023, and it had taken about a year to put together and work out how to get it into the hands of people who might read it.

Naturally, I was on a high and felt a sense of relief and satisfaction. But it begged the question, "What's next, Smithy?" not intending at all to write straight away.

I wasn't prepared for the answer that popped into my head, but it became quite obvious that the Easter story published just before Christmas wasn't perfect timing for that book. Instead, it should have been the Christmas story.

And that's how it commenced!

The planning and inspiration for this book came during the Christmas 2023 festivities, which enabled me to capture the story of Jesus' birth again as it was retold in our churches and schools to wide audiences.

The Christmas event is quite a bit different to Easter, with the focus on Christmas Day turning into an outpouring of gifts from one person to another. I found there were few liturgical practices that help lead up to Christmas, unlike Easter which has Lent and the 14 Stations of the Cross and 14 Stations of the Light.

So I had to look at the Christmas story a bit differently.

This book puts together the prophecies that point towards the birth of Jesus Christ, and tries to provide a historical and personal backdrop surrounding the Biblical promises that were given. By seeing through the eyes of the people in these stories and using the approach in our modern society of an advent calendar, I have attempted to assemble a contemporary Christian book that helps us to take time to reflect on the need for a Saviour.

The story starts with Eve, having been bitten by the effects of sin and throwing the world off course from the original order that God had created. We then follow the events of history through numerous promises of God to people who would inherit the promises and be part of the lineage and storyline of Christ.

Out of respect for modern Jewish custom, I've put a dash through the 'o' in the word for God, represented as G-d but pronounced as God like we would normally say it. I used the same technique in *Via Crucis Via Lucis,* which is intended to get us thinking in the culture and timeframe of the people of Israel rather than looking through Western eyes. Please don't take offence at this simple writing technique.

Whether you are a believer in Jesus or not, the Christmas season is likely to have some level of impact on you. Most people will buy a gift for someone, or themselves; shops will be open late to provide for last minute gifts; and you are likely to be called to work extra time (if in the retail industry) or forced to take time off with the rest of the company during the Christmas–New Year period. What I'm saying is that you are likely to be affected by modern Christmas celebrations or holidays, whether intended or not.

What are you planning to celebrate this Christmas?

If you will allow me to walk with you, then I encourage you to take the time to read through the promises of God and celebrate the birth of Jesus.

Blessings in Christ,

Brother Brad Smith

Advent 1:

The Curse

And I will cause hostility between you and the woman,

and between your offspring and her offspring.

He will strike your head,

and you will strike his heel.

Genesis 3:15

ᴖEve's Storyᴗ

Adam and I played in The Garden many times before, and today was another gift from G-d.

Light filled the atmosphere bringing everything to life. Trees swayed in melody as if dancing to an unseen rhythm, the creation itself buzzing with vibrancy and brilliance.

Plants and insects created an abundance of energy and an enchanted intimacy with each other, building a fascinating stage of entertainment and amusement.

Observing these scenes filled our senses with deep satisfaction and delight at the handiwork of our Creator, and brought us contentment in each part of the day.

It was bliss.

The spectacular display each night poured forth speech from the brilliance of the stars scattered throughout the heavens. Their magnificent splendour told the story of the world that we were part of, a world which we could never fully grasp.

Life was beautiful.

Everything I could ever wish for was right here: the man of my dreams, to be dancing with all of creation; every longing of my soul was satisfied.

I could not ask for anything more.

As we played, my eye caught sight of the Tree. We'd been warned about it, the Lord had strictly cautioned us not to eat its fruit or we would die.

The fruit is something that I'd not taken the time to observe, but the restriction kept my mind alert whenever we came near the Tree. As a result we had hardly played in the centre of The Garden.

Today was different, for some reason we were being drawn in. There was a moment that the song of creation seemed to pause, holding its breath while I heard my name being called, though it wasn't my husband's voice.

Mother.

I turned towards the Tree and listened closely.

Mother …

There it was again.

MOTHER EVE.

The Tree seemed to draw me towards it, bringing me closer. My curiosity was aroused. Unlike other times when I knew not of its threatening beauty, the Tree and its' fruit captivated the fullness of my mind and emotions.

I needed to step closer to experience it more fully, so I moved under the aromatic branches. The smell of cinnamon fragrance emanated from the Tree, combined with a mixture of other spices, which lifted my soul with delight as my body absorbed the scents.

Oh my!

This was unlike any other tree in the Garden, its radiant fruit hung within reach and begged me to hold it. Like the speech from the starry hosts, the Tree seemed to be calling me and would not allow me to look away.

I was captivated by its beauty and the opportunity it presented. Just being in this area gave me the feeling of awe.

The Tree continued to speak, as though offering a deeper knowledge than what we had already received from the Lord at creation.

"I can make you wise, to know the difference between good and evil." The words echoed in my mind, "make you wise … wise … wise …"

A strong connection formed between the fruit and my mind — in fact my *entire being* — wanted to know this sacred bond. Why was I unable to let it go?

I couldn't.

Reaching up, I took the glistening fruit and held it closely to my chest. Just holding it brought me a sense of power. The fullness of the beauty of what I held in my hands totally enthralled me

The voice in the Tree continued, so I leered in to locate the speaker.

It took a small while, my eyes having to refocus to distinguish the reptile from the camouflaged foliage that it used to cover itself.

"Did G-d say …?" came the slippery tone.

"Did G-d say that you shouldn't eat from any tree of the Garden?"

My mind raced for answers.

Of course we could eat of any of the fruit trees — we'd been delighted with their flavour, their touch, and their effects on our bodies for as long as we'd eaten them. They rejuvenated us physically and emotionally.

No, there was nothing wrong with any of the fruit trees.

"Only of the one Tree, this one, in the centre of the Garden, are we to abstain from eating — and touching — the fruit, lest we die."

My own words shook me, realising that I stood under the Tree, holding the forbidden fruit. And yet I felt strangely, strongly, satisfyingly connected to it.

The voice continued, challenging the words I'd believed for so long, "You won't die. Rather, your eyes will be opened to both good and evil. You will be like G-d!"

The words sunk deep, and my heart pounded to think that there was more to this incredible reality than we had come to experience. I questioned the validity of my thinking and the bounds that the Lord had set in place concerning this Tree, and its fruit. Perhaps it would be okay, just this once?

Why would G-d keep this wisdom from us?

I took a long gaze at the object in my hands; it glistened in the light of day. Its beautiful radiance filled me with delight just to hold it, but if we were to experience its nourishing taste then it will change our level of understanding and we can become like G-d Himself.

There was no reason to hold us back now.

Glancing over my shoulder towards my husband for his approval, I peeled off the skin and took the first bite.

A sacred exchange took place.

Wow.

WOW!

This tasted better than anything I had eaten from the Garden before!

My entire being resonated with the rhythm of creation; my vision immediately broadened across the extent of the universe. My soul exploded with satisfaction as the effects of the fruit took effect on my body.

"So this is what was being held back from me?"
I quizzed, smirking. With delight, I passed on the
fruit to my husband. He accepted, and ate.

Just like me, Adam entered into a trance-like
state of wonder and amazement. We could see
the outer rim of the universe start to peel away.
Everything we knew — or believed — had been
sheltered from our eyes. And now our vision
started to expand infinitely beyond what we could
see and feel.

The foreground started to blur; the Tree, the
fruit, the serpent. We were being drawn upwards
into the sky.

As the fruit dropped from our hands to the
ground, our bodies seemed to fly past myriads of
stars into the outer reaches of space.

Certainly we were becoming wise. This was clearly
hidden from our eyes, and we had not seen it.

We were becoming 'gods', just as the serpent
had said.

Passing through the heavens, we finally came to
a stop and looked down towards the Garden and
the Tree where we had been standing. And there
we were: staring at ourselves from the outer most
reaches of the galaxy.

But how could it be that we were in two places at once? We felt the physical presence of our bodies in front of the Tree, and yet our spirits were away in the heavens.

As we circled the scene from above, a darkness began to fill our bodies below.

What?

WAIT!

We don't know darkness. And yet, here it is.

It felt like a door had been left open and a draft had come in, creating a cold breeze inside my bones and proceeding up my back.

The cold flushed through my body in waves, chilling my emotions, and started to take control of my entire being.

What is happening?

The feeling didn't go away, it shook me from the inside.

Then a shockwave — a resounding gong, bellowed from the core of my being throughout the universe. This was a declaration that an eternal exchange had taken place.

I fell to the ground, shaking. My spirit returned but the iridescent glow of my body started to fade.

No — it *disappeared.*

Instead of being covered with the soft embodiment of physical luminescence from a godly glow, I stared at my now naked body that lacked the original G-d given heavenly covering and protection.

Rain showered above me, and a cold darkness overtook me, making me shiver.

I needed to hide.

The creation had looked on to witness this event — summoned by my exclamation of fear. Now, instead of being a superior race like G-d — full of wisdom and knowledge — they witnessed a pathetic ball of mortal flesh that became insignificant in the totality of life.

I was afraid.

Tears welled down my face.

Dark clouds filled the sky.

My husband, nearby, also ashamed and disgraced.

We sought refuge from the nearby trees, and
robbed the fig of its leaves to cover ourselves
from the stares of creation.

We were outcasts.

Cut off, and cursed from G-d.

What have we done?

And could this be fixed?

Advent 2:
The Priest

And Melchizedek, the king of Salem and a priest of
G-d Most High,

brought Abram some bread and wine.

Melchizedek blessed Abram with this blessing:

'Blessed be Abram by G-d Most High,

Creator of heaven and earth.

And blessed be G-d Most High,

who has defeated your enemies for you."

Then Abram gave Melchizedek a tenth of all the goods he
had recovered.

Genesis 14:18-20

⁓*Melchizedek's Story*⁓

People in the area knew me as the priest of
G-d Most High, a title that I received from the
cleansing rituals I had performed for many years.
The history of my life and the record of my birth
is obscure. Perhaps there is a reason why I was
called into this position, hidden from public life
until the right time.

It has been my privilege to bring praise, honour
and blessing to my Creator G-d for many years.
Just as Abel who gave the best portions of the
firstborn lambs from his flocks, there has been
nothing more pleasing to me than to see the
smoke of my offerings be accepted as a pleasing
sacrifice to the Almighty.

And just like Abel, the Lord openly accepted
my gifts and sacrifices each time I came to Him.

Daily I pursue our friendship and I am blessed with His wonderful presence wherever I go.

The Lord is always with me.

But not so with the nations that surround me. They do not share the love for G-d that they see I have, nor do they desire a relationship with the Creator. I am careful to live righteously, for that is what my G-d requires of me. And it is my joy to be able to serve Him in this way.

The people of these nations know that I am not only high priest, but also king of Salem, the city of peace, and yet they don't want to follow after G-d. In fact, they avoid having anything to do with me, or the city I govern.

After the great flood, Noah's sons went their ways and divided the land among themselves, according to the Table of Nations. Ham took the area of Egypt, along with the land of Canaan. Shem received the portion of land to the east of the Red Sea and north, known as the land of Uzal. Japheth took land in the north, that is, the land of Lud. Together their lands intersected in the north where the head of the four rivers meet. This was the beginning of life after the deluge, the beginning of the new creation.

My city Salem was between the land settlements of Shem and Ham, lying east of the land of Canaan. It was during this time that the surrounding nations begun to be a stench in the nostrils of my G-d, with their constant bickering towards each other. Even though they all descended from their father Noah, there was no way that they could get on with each other. While there was unrest elsewhere, under my leadership and authority our city experienced peace. I attribute this directly to my role as king and priest to G-d Most High.

In time, war broke out amongst the brothers.

Ham's descendants, the kings of the west, refused to pay tribute to the kings of the east, and as a result Shem's descendants came against the kings of the west, four against five. The kings of the west weren't able to stand up to the kings of the east, and they carried away everything that was part of the city. Unfortunately, this also included the nephew of a man named Abram, who was taken into captivity as part of the plunder.

Abram burned with indignant rage against the kings of the east as they clearly had no regard for the foreigners in the camp. Drawing his armed forces, he took off in pursuit. Having attacked and overcome them, he brought back his nephew Lot, along with the women and other foreigners, and all Lot's possessions.

The battle of the kings was settled.

The situation was being brought back to peace, and I recognised that Abram had done this to honour G-d by rescuing his nephew Lot from a life of slavery.

Putting on my priestly garments, I headed out to meet Abram. My emotions bubbled high that someone had taken a stand against the nations for all their ungodly actions that they had done to each other for many years. I wanted to assure him that what he had done was a pleasing aroma to G-d Most High and I was intent to bring Abram into the presence of the Lord, so I packed the bread and wine.

As I was on the way, the king of Sodom drew near to pay homage to Abram for bringing back his people from the war, and offered him all the goods that he had brought back. "Just give me the persons, and take the goods for yourself."

Looking to me, Abram sensed that this was not an offer of grace from the defeated king. According to Akkadian rule at that time, Abram had the right to keep all the people and goods for himself. This was also stated as acceptable conduct in the Code of Hammurabi. The king of Sodom really wasn't offering Abram anything!

Abram replied: "O King of Sodom, I have raised my hand to the Lord G-d Most High, the possessor of heaven and earth. I have vowed to take nothing from you, not even a thread of a sandal strap. I will take nothing that is yours, lest you might say, 'I have made Abram rich!'"

The king looked to the ground, not able to take in these words.

Abram continued, "I will take only what my young warriors have already eaten, and I request that you give a fair share of the goods to my allies: Aner, Eshcol and Mamre; let them take their portion."

At this, the king went away to split up the spoils as directed.

"Abram!" I called.

He turned to look at me, our eyes fixated together in a knowing, friendly embrace.

Bringing the bread and wine, I set it up on a table for us to enjoy fellowship.

Here we sat for precious moments together in the presence of the Lord. There was something special that I received, which I wanted to pass onto this man of righteousness before he left.

Finishing the elements, I lowered my hands onto the shoulders of my friend, and declared this blessing,

> "Blessed be Abram by G-d Most High,
> Creator of heaven and earth.
> And blessed be G-d Most High,
> Who has defeated your enemies for you."

Abram bathed in the divine blessing being poured upon him, taking in the fullness of these words that reached deep into his spirit and touched the depths of his soul. Tears of joy flowed down my new friends face.

We finished after a short while, and then it was time to depart. Our time was fruitful, the blessing carried an eternal weight that rested on him and his family forever.

Turning to me, Abram brought me a reciprocal blessing, "Melchizedek, I bless you with a tenth of everything that I have recovered." And he ordered the young men to set apart the holy gift as a sign of our friendship.

"Abram!" I called, as he was leaving.

His face and eyes shone with the peace of righteousness. I knew that we had a life-long friendship, the covenantal blessing and tithe brought that together during our time of fellowship.

"Abram, although I am known as the priest and king of Salem, I promise you that I will not be the last. There is another coming after me and He will fulfill all that was promised to you!"

Advent 3:
The Covenant

But G-d replied,

'No—Sarah, your wife,

will give birth to a son for you.

You will name him Isaac,

and I will confirm my covenant with him

and his descendants as an everlasting covenant."

Genesis 17:19

⌒Sarah's Story⌒

I was in the tent when the men arrived, it was the hottest part of the day. Flies buzzed annoyingly. I swiped them clear of my face as I peered through the tent opening to see what was happening outside. I was not quite prepared to entertain foreign visitors right now, at ninety years of age the heat was getting to me and I needed a rest. We would need to get the Egyptian slave out to help, if anything was needed.

My husband was in the shade of his tent, and looking up he noticed the three men approaching. We had not seen the likes of them around here before. I was curious as to why he bowed low to the ground while approaching them so timidly — were they men of stature? Sometimes my husband does the strangest things, but indeed there was something about these men that caused him to seek their favour. What could it possibly be? I leaned in towards the edge of the tent to overhear the conversation, if possible.

"My lord," Abraham sought the attention of the men. "If it pleases you, stop here for a while. Rest in the shade of this tree while water is brought to wash your feet. And since you've honoured your servant with this visit, let me prepare some food to refresh you before you continue on your journey."

"Alright then — do as you have said," they responded.

The requests came quick. Urgency was in his voice. Abraham did not want to let the men go without blessing them in some way. He sought their favour with the treatment he would normally give to a foreign king.

"Sarah — take three seahs of our best flour, knead it into dough, and bake bread." I knew this request couldn't be ignored; he had that look about him that insisted that this was a command and not simply an appeal. Glumly I set to work to bake the bread, and set up a fire out the back.

Abraham ran to the herd and chose a tender young calf, and gave it to the servant with the request, "Hagar — take this calf, and prepare it for our guests." This was a messy job, and would require both her and her son to prepare the meat, then roast it on a fire.

When the food was ready, he set it before them along with yoghurt and milk, and waited in the shade of the trees while they ate.

This was not an ordinary meal.

It was prepared in haste for three passing men whom we did not know, my husband treating them as though they were kings. Receiving the food from our hands, they ate in silence. Their faces carried a look of seriousness and concern, which made me nervous.

Who were they?
What did they want?
Why is my husband playing up to them?

I preferred to hide myself in the tent out of sight, though not out of earshot.

With the meal finished, one of them asked, "Where is Sarah, your wife?"

I didn't want to be involved.
How did they know my name?
What do they want with me?

My suspicions arose, fear stirred my soul into a panic; I crouched lower in the tent to avoid any form of contact.

"She's inside," Abraham replied.

There he goes again!
Why can't he keep to his own business, and leave me out of whatever is going on here?

I'm getting flustered now.

I was not only embarrassed, but almost angry that my husband was drawn to entertain them.

In any case, I was not leaving my tent.

Then one of them said, "I will return to you about this time next year, and your wife, Sarah, will have a son!"

I stopped to catch my breath.

My heart jumped a beat out of rhythm.

And my silent anger broke into sarcasm.

Was I hearing right?
'Sarah will have a son.'

Surely they got that wrong.
*Can't they see that I'm a worn out old woman, with no
chance of ever having children now?*

But it's not just me; my husband's strength peaked
many years ago. Back when we were younger, G-d
had made him a promise, affirming, "No, your
servant will not be your heir, for you will have a
son of your own who will be your heir.' The Lord
had said, 'Look up into the sky and count the
stars if you can. That's how many descendants
you will have!"

But the years passed, and this so-called promise
was fruitless. How was G-d going to fulfil His
word when our bodies were now well past the age
of child-bearing?

I had thought that G-d intended us to fulfil the
promise by our own creativity.

Maybe we needed to help G-d bring it about?

I did not want my husband to see this promise
broken, or to miss out on the chance of
fatherhood. So I gave him my Egyptian slave,
and she bore him a son, Ishmael. That was twelve
years ago. Now he's approaching one hundred,
and not getting any younger. And that promise is
a distant memory.

Right now, I am well past the age of child bearing. It has been the scorn of my life as I experienced the humiliation of being called 'barren' from not only friends and strangers, but also family.

And what's worse, that slave — Hagar — has treated me with contempt since the day she had the child. She paraded around me in a way that over-stated her role and position in this family. It cut me to tears.

Now these men arrived, and having had food prepared for them, came out with an absurd statement. It made no sense to me at all and I felt worse when they said it. They obviously weren't aware of the ridicule I received over the course of my life, and my resulting pain.

Who do these men think they are?

Do they know my body better than me?

If they knew, then they wouldn't be making this claim.

A son?
Really?
From this *good-as-dead* body?

My sarcasm and frustration broke into a personal bout of laughter at the thought of how this body would rise from the dead to have a child, breaking the airy gathering outside the tent.

One of the men peered towards me, and asked, "Why did Sarah laugh? Why did she say, 'Can an old woman like me have a baby?' Is anything too hard for the Lord? I will return about this time next year, and Sarah will have a son.'"

At this, my body filled with guilt, anxiety and fear. My mind clouded by panic.

I pulled back the curtain of the tent to enforce my position, stating to the men, "But I didn't laugh."

The Lord said, "No, but you did laugh."

As I recall these memories from twelve months ago, I again break into a quiet laugh, holding my newborn son Isaac in my arms.

The covenant *is* real, and I am blessed to be part of it. The episode left me pondering.

Who is this son of promise?
Why is he so special?
What plans does G-d have for him?

Advent 4:
The Blessing

I will surely bless you

and make your descendants

as numerous as the stars in the sky

and as the sand on the seashore.

Your descendants will take possession
of the cities of their enemies,

and through your offspring
all nations on earth will be blessed,

because you have obeyed me.

Genesis 22:17–18

Abraham's Story

We had already travelled for three days, just the four of us, heading to a place of worship for a special sacrifice. It was not a place that we had known, for the path was not beaten and the location was remote.

The mountainous terrain ahead came into view just like the vision I received while in prayer a week earlier. The sacrifice was to be officiated on top of a mountain in the land of Moriah.

Turning to my servants, I motioned that my son and I would be traversing the mountain to sacrifice a burnt offering there. "Stay with the donkey while I take the boy with me to worship, then we will come back to you."

The wood had been cut prior to our journey, and we loaded it onto the back of my son, Isaac, to be carried up the mountain. He was 100 years younger than myself, being 13 years of age, he was a lot fitter and stronger for the journey ahead. I pocketed the knife, and carried the fire with me. It was time to leave.

The journey up the slope introduced some delays, causing us to stop and catch our breath intermittently; this gave me a few additional precious hours of personal time with my son.

This wasn't an ordinary journey.

It was a journey of faith and obedience.

And I was depending on the Lord's favour to reward my actions.

Although I was nervous, I was committed to obey this part of the vision: *to offer my son as a sacrifice of worship on the hill top.*

No-one else knew about the pact that I had agreed to. And this was quite intentional — I didn't want the disapproval from others to affect my call to obedience, lest I stray from the call and fail to respond to this request from the Lord.

It tore me up inside to think that the promised blessing was to come through my son Isaac, from the wife I loved, Sarah, and not through her

Egyptian slave, Hagar. And yet, on this journey I had resolved to obey the voice of the Lord; whereas I had previously listened to the voice of my wife and received my first-born son, Ishmael, through her slave Hagar.

Determined to obey, I considered that perhaps there would be a way that G-d can raise the dead.

Even so, the sacrifice meant that the promise I had received was being tested. We were starting to approach the clearing where we could build the altar.

"Father," came the inquisitive voice of my son. "Father, the fire and wood are here, but where is the lamb for the burnt offering?"

The seal on the scroll of my secret agenda was being prised open, and I could not let this query side-track what I was asked to do. "Isaac, G-d Himself will provide the lamb for the burnt offering. All has been prepared ahead of time."

Trusting, we gathered some unhewn rocks to build an altar and laid the wood on it. Looking to the right and left around the nearby shrubs and bushes, the lamb was nowhere to be seen. An eerie wind blew while I decided what steps to take next.

When all was in place, I turned to my son, and with tear filled eyes explained the sacrifice that I had been asked to perform. I was not expecting his response, but we embraced and cried and said our good-byes.

I didn't know why G-d would ask this of me. I only knew that He wanted me to be willing and obedient.

"Father, do what you have been asked to do. I submit myself to the Lord, and your hand."

Removing my waist belt, I bound my son onto the altar, placing him on top of the wood.

There was no struggle.
Everything was in place, but my heart was racing.
I was facing a crisis of obedience.

How could G-d expect to bring about the fulfilment of the promise if the son of promise was to die? He had said, *'Sarah will bear you a son, and you will call him Isaac. I will establish my covenant with him as an everlasting covenant for his descendants after him.'*

It was time.

Reaching for my knife, I took it from the sheath and raised it to the sky. My heart drummed loudly in my chest, causing my hands to shake. With the knife poised, I looked up to heaven and prayed, asking that G-d make this an acceptable sacrifice.

I had done all things that I knew was right in order to obey the voice of the Lord.

Looking down at my son, our eyes locked for the last time. This was our final good-byes. His eyes reflected a peace that accepted the fate that had been assigned to him. He allowed me to practice obedience, even to the point of offering himself up as a sacrifice to G-d.

Good-bye, son.

No more waiting.

"ABRAHAM! ABRAHAM!"

A voice from heaven called. It was an angel.

Hesitant, I looked up. "Here I am"

"Abraham, do not lay a hand on the boy. Do not do anything to him. Now I know that you fear G-d, because you have not withheld from me your son, your only son."

My eyes filled with tears. Breaking down in front of the altar, I wept.

Thank you G-D!

It took me some time to compose myself, as I loosened the bond that held Isaac in place, and prised him off the altar. Together we embraced for some time, and wiped back the tears from each other's face.

Thank you for giving me back my son.

Looking up we saw a young ram caught in a bush nearby. It's horns had become entangled in the thicket and was not able to move.

Thank you for providing the sacrificial lamb.

Together we brought the ram over to the altar, and sacrificed it there as a burnt offering to the Lord.

After we finished worshiping the Lord, the angel called out a second time.

> "I swear by myself, declares the Lord,
> that because you have done this and have not
> withheld your son, your only son,
> I will surely bless you and make your
> descendants
> as numerous as the stars in the sky
> and as the sand on the seashore.
> Your descendants will take possession of the
> cities of their enemies.
> Through your offspring all nations on earth
> will be blessed, because you have obeyed me."

We called that place "Jehovah Jireh — The Lord Will Provide".

But what we didn't know was just how significant that sacrifice of obedience was to be for future generations.

Advent 5:
The Dream

Your descendants will be as numerous
as the dust of the earth!

They will spread out in all directions —
to the west and the east,
to the north and the south.

And all the families of the earth will be blessed
through you and your descendants.

Genesis 28:14

~Jacob's Story~

It was now *my turn* to find a wife.

I was longing for the right woman who would stand by my side, to share my life and dreams. Together we would inherit the promises made by G-d to my grandfather Abraham and my father Isaac.

Those bold and precious promises were confirmed through mighty miracles and actions by the G-d we serve. I was careful to walk in keeping with the covenant that we had received, and avoid falling into error like my brother who married foreign women. This surely hurt my father and mother, bringing shame to our family.

I realised that this was not likely an easy task, she had to be *the one*.

The story of how my father and mother met was nothing short of unusual. They retold it thousands of times as they put me to sleep each night; their eyes lovingly danced towards each other to show the special bond they shared. And they wanted me to be sure that my future wife would be able to carry the responsibility, along with the blessing, that we received.

They pressed upon me that marriage was a special covenant and commitment between two people, for life. It not only carried on the family traditions, but also the blessings received by our ancestors.

But when my brother married *without consideration* outside our family clan, my father was displeased, and this made me cautious. Esau, my 'older' brother, though only by a few minutes, as we were twins, had taken women from the land of Canaan as wives. Father had expressed *in no uncertain terms* that they repulsed him. He did not want them, or their children, in our family line. They were not to be part of the promises, and would never share in the inheritance.

So I was careful to listen to my father's voice.

"Jacob, please take my advice when finding a wife." Isaac started.

I moved in to hear his words.

"You must not take any of these Canaanite women. Instead, go at once to Paddan-aram, to the house of your grandfather Bethuel, and marry one of your uncle Laban's daughters."

Sensing that I had accepted his words, he continued, "Son, now I have a blessing to pass onto you, before you leave."

Drawing near, I closed my eyes as he rested his hands on my head and shoulders, his voice was firm and assuring:

> "May the Almighty G-d bless you
>   and give you many children.
> May your descendants multiply
>   and become many nations!
> May G-d pass on to you and your descendants
>   the blessings he promised to Abraham.
> May you own this land where you are now
>   living as a foreigner, for G-d gave this land
>   to Abraham."

As he lifted his hands, I felt a glorious presence came to rest on me. I let it settle for around ten minutes before moving from my position, and together we embraced.

With fathers' blessing, I packed and headed off
with family servants to my mothers' land to
search for my uncle Laban in the northern region,
a week's walk from where we were living now.

At sundown we reached the hill at Luz. It was a
good place to stop, so we set up camp before it
got too dark.

Exhausted from the journey, I found a large rock
and lay down to rest for the night. As I drifted
into a deep sleep, a large stairway appeared before
me, reaching up into heaven. The angels of G-d
were ascending and descending the stairway.

What could this mean?

As I rose to the top of the stairway, I met the
Lord, and He spoke to me, saying,

> "I am the Lord, the G-d of your grandfather
> Abraham, and the G-d of your father, Isaac.
>
> The ground you are lying on belongs to you.
> I am giving it to you and your descendants.
>
> Your descendants will be as numerous as the
> dust of the earth!
> They will spread out in all directions—to the
> west and the east, to the north and the south.

And all the families of the earth will be
blessed through you and your descendants.
What's more, I am with you, and I will
protect you wherever you go.

One day I will bring you back to this land.
I will not leave you until I have finished
giving you everything I have promised you."

The weight of heavenly glory fell upon me
again as I awoke. My whole being dripped with
a substance like honey from the presence of the
Lord. My father's blessing did not simply come
from an earthly perspective, it now came directly
from the Lord of heaven Himself.

*Surely the Lord is in this place, and I have not been aware
of it!*

A holy fear struck me to my core. This encounter
was not simply a dream. I entered into the
heavenly environment juxtaposed against the
backdrop of earth. This encounter was the
fulfilment of the promises made to my father and
grandfather, and now being passed on to me.

What an awesome place this is!

Although it was dark, I wasn't able to fall back
to sleep. The dream continued in the present,

energising my spirit and I kept breathing in the heavenly atmosphere.

I wanted to mark this place as a tribute, a memorial pillar that would be remembered for generations to come. Calling the other men to me, we lifted the stone into position and set it upright. The effect was that it could be seen from a distance away from the top of this hill, and would be a fitting monument to my Lord and G-d.

This is none other than the house of G-d, the very gateway to heaven.

Picking up a flask of olive oil, I poured it on top of the rock, emptying the last of it to cover the entire pillar.

There, a fitting tribute to the promises that I had just received.

During the anointing of the stone pillar, I offered up my own vows to the Lord:

> "If G-d will indeed be with me
>   and protect me on this journey,
> and if he will provide me with food and clothing,
> and if I return safely to my father's home,
> then the Lord will certainly be my G-d.
>
> And this memorial pillar I have set up
>   will become a place for worshiping G-d,

> and I will present to G-d a tenth
> of everything he gives me."

From that time on, I called the place Bethel, because it had become a house of G-d.

With confidence we packed up, and continued north to find the woman who would become my wife.

But would she realise G-d's calling on my life?

Would she want to be part of it?

Advent 6:

The Sceptre

The sceptre will not depart from Judah,

nor the ruler's staff from his descendants,

until the coming of the one to whom it belongs,

the one whom all nations will honour.

Genesis 49:10

~Tamar's Story~

This was a sad day for everyone. All the family had been called to gather around the bedside of our patriarch Jacob, for what would be his last words to the Twelve. We all knew why we were there, and the feelings of grief from his impending death were shared equally amongst us.

I had been asked to wait outside until the time was ready for Jacob to pass on his blessing to Judah, who was not only my father-in-law, *but also* the father of my twins Perez and Zerah. Due to this known circumstance in the family, it was awkward for me to be with him by the bedside at the time, unlike the rest of the family who were by nature of the bloodline of grandfather Abraham.

My life has been populated with unwanted loss, and I was not unfamiliar with rejection and grief.

Judah's oldest son, Er, was my first husband.
Our family was expected to live under the
patriarchal promises as part of G-d's covenant
with Abraham. However my husband despised
the rules that we were expected to follow and
instead followed the rebellious teaching of his
mother, who was a Canaanite I believe he died an
untimely death as a result. I had become a widow
before we could even start a family.

As was our custom, Er's brother Onan was
obligated to marry me in order keep the lineage
of his brother alive. He was the first born in the
family. Reluctantly he took on this responsibility,
and I married into the family a second time,
though it was more of a cultural obligation than
his desire for me. Whenever we came together,
Onan would withdraw and I was unable to get
pregnant. He wanted his first child to be his very
own heir, rather than surrender this to his elder
brother. Onan's disregard to honour his brother
and the law was a sign of being unfaithful. It left
me without child, and his brother without an heir,
and in the course of time Onan also passed away
in an untimely manner.

While my dreams and expectations of starting
a family had been one of joy and excitement,
over the years I could sense my chances were

diminishing, and instead felt as though a curse had attached itself to me instead: the scourge of two men that died while being married to me.

By nature of the law, I was expecting to marry the next son of Judah, Shelah. He was not at all of age or maturity to marry, though one day he would be able to fulfil this dutiful role and take me to be his wife. Though it would be many years later, if possible, making child bearing almost impossible for me. However this turned out not to be the case. Judah had feared that Shelah would be put to death like his brothers, so instead he insisted that I return to my own father's household until such time that Shelah was ready to marry. His words scorched my soul; nothing spoke louder than a failed widow that was to be returned to her father.

Scared and ashamed, under the advice of Judah, I returned home. The drab widows clothing served as a continual reminder of my loss, labelling me as a somewhat 'cursed' person in our society. Although the pain of my return caused me sorrow, my family were pleased to have their daughter back under the roof again and this gave me relief when I needed it the most.

In time I heard that my father-in-law had lost his wife, and they mourned for her during the traditional burial period. Judah had hastily taken a wife from Canaan without consideration or consultation with his father Jacob, but with her passing, this ended the family quarrels surrounding the situation that he had created.

During the course of time at my parents' house, I had been waiting for Shelah to come of age and it was now quite clear to me that Judah did not intend to carry out his stated intentions. So I remained without husband, with little chance of having a normal family. No-one wanted to marry a widow, especially since her two previous husbands had died through very unnatural means.

I was feeling desperate, neglected and forgotten.

Why was I being punished like this?

My sorrow and grief grew daily, my life's dreams and goals were quite simply unable to be fulfilled.

Word had got around that Judah was heading out of town to supervise the shearing of his sheep, and this meant that he had to travel through my village on the way. Knowing that Judah had been released from his marital rites, I knew that he would have felt somewhat needy. *Very needy.*

Would this be a way for me to fulfil the responsibilities of his family line?

Taking off my mourning clothes, I slipped into something light and attractive as a sign to say that I was 'available'. With a veil over my face I sat on the roadside at the entrance to the town. Soon enough, Judah appeared with his friend Hirah, and approached me.

"Excuse me," he motioned, "are you …?"

I swallowed a shallow gulp and took a gasp, responding with a simple, "Yes, sir. How much will you pay me?"

Judah consulted with Hirah, and promised, "I'll send you a goat from my flock."

"Ok. But what can you leave me as a guarantee that you will do as you say, until I receive it from you?" I quizzed.

"I'm not sure — what do you suggest?" was his reply.

I needed a valid form of identity, items that would clearly belong to its owner. "How about your signet ring, and cord, and the staff that you are carrying?"

"Agreed."

The deal was done. We quietly slipped into a friends borrowed room, and he left.

About three months later I became aware that I was pregnant.

The news travelled back to Judah (who was a recognised prince in the area) and it was reported saying, "Tamar, your daughter-in-law, has acted like a prostitute. And now, because of this, she's pregnant." The news angered Judah, and his so-called righteous indignation incited the community against me.

A heated mob of men stormed upon my parents' house to retrieve me, eager to fulfil the commands of the man that they looked up to, the pillar of their community.

"Bring her out, and let her be burned!" Judah demanded.

Strong men grabbed me by the arms, leveraging me out of the door and into the street.

Before I was ejected from the house, I asked one of the men to closely look at what I was holding. "The man who owns these things made me pregnant. Look closely. Whose seal and cord and staff are these?" There was a pause while the items were taken outside.

My vindication was at hand.

Judah recognized them immediately.

His actions returned to haunt him like dreams that he was trying to escape from.

> The guilt of denying me the right to marry
>   his son Shelah, and produce an heir.
> The guilt of pursuing his own pleasure
>   while calling an end to my own life.
> And the guilt of marrying a Canaanite woman,
>   when he clearly understood that
>   *they were not to marry these women.*

The emotional load that he was carrying was too much to keep in. The realisation that he was not able to punish me for the things that he had done was overwhelming.

He broke down, weeping in front of my pursuers, and confessed. "She is more righteous than I am, because I didn't arrange for her to marry my son Shelah."

This admission brought healing and relief to my aching soul, and similarly I broke into a fountain of tears. For many years I had tortured myself believing that I was the problem, and I was the outcast; that it was all my fault for not marrying the right man or bearing children.

This release set me free from the guilt that
plagued me.

I was restored.

As I recalled the years of grief and suffering,
Judah and I were called in, to catch the words of
the blessing.

Israel proceeded.

"Judah, your brothers will praise you.
    You will grasp your enemies by the neck.
    All your relatives will bow before you.

Judah, my son, is a young lion
    that has finished eating its prey.
Like a lion he crouches and lies down;
    like a lioness—who dares to rouse him?

The sceptre will not depart from Judah,
    nor the ruler's staff from his descendants,
until the coming of the one
    to whom it belongs,
    the one whom all nations will honour."

Looking at my sons, I connected with Perez in
a gaze that captured the promise spoken by his
grandfather.

The sceptre will not depart from Judah, nor the rulers staff from his descendants, until the coming of the one to whom it belongs, the one whom all nations will honour.

Figuratively, Judah's staff *that I had received as a guarantee* was to be passed on to my children, and their children, and they would rule until the sceptre came to the one whom it belongs, *the one whom all nations will honour.*

That pointed to a time in the future for a coming king.

But when was this king to arrive?

And who would that king be?

Advent 7:
The Ruler

I see him, but not here and now.

I perceive him, but far in the distant future.

A star will rise from Jacob;

a sceptre will emerge from Israel.

It will crush the heads of Moab's people,

cracking the skulls of the people of Sheth.

Edom will be taken over,

and Seir, its enemy, will be conquered,

while Israel marches on in triumph.

A ruler will rise in Jacob

who will destroy the survivors of Ir.

Numbers 22:17–19

~Balak's Story~

"HOW DARE YOU?!"

I was furious, storming around the open air theatre that became the scene of our final encounter.

"BALAAM!" I strained my voice to keep it under control, trying to recompose myself.

"I CALLED YOU TO CURSE MY ENEMIES!"

Balaam was the most respected diviner in the land of Syria; his prophecies almost always came true, even from a young age. As a servant in the kings household, merely fifteen years old, he had grown powerful in witchcraft and caught the eye of King Angeas. A nearby king, King Zepho, had been entreating Angeas to come and wage war against the sons of Jacob that lived in Egypt, though Angeas was unwilling to entertain the idea.

After much badgering, Angeas finally consented to Zepho, agreeing to go to war. However he was first to consult the youthful Balaam to determine whether it was worth the effort.

With a set of wax figures, Balaam modelled the fight between King Zepho and the sons of Jacob in Egypt, consulting the powers of darkness about the battle. Under the incantation, Angeas' army fell by the sword at the hands of the sons of Jacob. This was a battle that they were not going to win.

As a result, Angeas despaired of the plan and did not go to war with Zepho, and the battle never eventuated. Egypt remained in peace.

"NOW GET OUT OF HERE!"

Balaam sourced his wisdom from spiritual powers to bring forth his prophecies. This gave him great status in the eyes of the ruling elite. In time he moved to Egypt, and dwelt with the nobles of the kings court, and all who encountered him coveted to learn his wisdom.

During the 130th year of Israel in Egypt, Pharoah dreamed that while he was sitting on his throne an old man stood before him. The old man held a set of merchant scales in his hands and hung them before Pharoah. He took all the elders and nobles and great men of Egypt, tied them together and put them on one side of the scales. On the other side he placed a milking goat, merely a kid, which outweighed them all.

Pharoah was disturbed by the dream, and having called his enchanters, wise men and magicians he sought an answer, but they couldn't interpret it. Finally he called in Balaam and asked, "What does this mean?"

Balaam responded, saying, "This means nothing less than a great evil will spring up against Egypt in the latter days, for a son will be born to Israel who will destroy all Egypt and its inhabitants and bring forth the children of Israel from Egypt with a mighty hand."

Understanding that the interpretation of the dream was valid, Pharoah grew afraid, his face darkened. "Then what shall we do?"

Calling his counsellors, they said to do this or to do that, but it did not seem to please the king, or provide a pathway for victory over the Israelites.

Again, turning back to Balaam, Pharoah asked, "Then what shall we do?"

Balaam replied, "Of all that the king has counselled against the Hebrews, they will be delivered, and the king will not be able to prevail over them with any counsel. Remember that their G-d prevailed for them through fire, from the sword, and from hard labour."

Balaam took a deep breath before uttering his next words of wisdom, knowing that the future of Egypt relied on what he would proclaim.

"If it please the king, let him order that all their children which shall be born from this day forward, be thrown into the water. This way you can wipe away their name from the face of the earth. For none of them, nor of their fathers, were tried in this manner."

Balaam's words pleased the king and the princes, and they decreed this word to the people of Israel. A proclamation was issued, and a law was made throughout the land of Egypt, saying, *Every male child born to the Hebrews from this day forward shall be thrown into the water.*

Pharaoh called all his servants, with these instructions. "Go now and seek throughout the land of Goshen where the children of Israel are, and see that every son born to the Hebrews be cast into the river, but every daughter you shall let live."

Pharaoh ordered his officers to go daily into the land to Goshen to seek the newborn male children of Israel. When they had sought and found one, they took it from its mother by force, and threw it into the river, but the female children they left with its mother.

"AND GO BACK HOME!"

The young child Moses grew up in the household of Pharoah, as a son to the kings daughter Bathia. The Lord gave Moses favour in the eyes of Pharoah, and before all his servants, and in front of all the people of Egypt. Everyone loved Moses exceedingly, the child prince of Egypt. He was clothed in royal purple and grew up among the children of the king.

One day Moses travelled through the land of Goshen and saw his own people, the children of Israel, in hard labour and with shortness of breath. He enquired, "Why is this burden upon you each day?"

The people stopped, and shared with Moses all the counsel that Balaam had instructed the king concerning them. "Before you were born, Pharoah listened to Balaam and burdened us with heavy loads to build the stately palace that you are in."

"Also," they shared, "when you were a mere infant in the palace, we had heard that you took the crown from the kings head and placed it on your own. This made the king furious, and Balaam said to slay you with the sword."

"What happened after that?" Moses enquired.

"Balaam sought the treaty of the king by using his special magic, to determine if his actions were worthy of death. He proposed a test: place an onyx stone and a burning coal in front of the child Moses. Balaam said, 'If he reaches out to grab the onyx stone then we will know that he stretched out his hand knowingly to take the kings crown. However if he grabs the fiery coal, then we will know that his actions were innocent and did not intend to take the crown from the kings head.'"

"As they placed the stone and the coal before you, an angel of the Lord took your hand and brought the coal to your mouth, which burnt your lips and tongue. This is why your words are spoken with a slur and are hard to hear at times."

Hearing this, Moses was angry that Balaam was allowed to remain in the kings palace, and sought to kill him day by day. As a result, Balaam left

Egypt and fled back to the land of Cush with his two sons.

"I PROMISED TO REWARD YOU RICHLY."

Balak was king over the land of Moab, and had grown increasingly nervous about the onward progression of the people of Israel, who passed triumphantly through Jericho crushing their walls to powder, defeating kings Sihon of Bashan and Og of the Amorites. With the Lord's help, the Israelites had no fear and they conquered these lands with robust victories.

"If they continue like this, my people won't survive," he feared. The people of Moab had grown increasingly afraid of them, which was disturbing.

King Balak sought to change this, and sent messengers to Balaam with a large financial reward if he would come to curse the Israelites.

Balak was insistent. "Look, a vast horde of people has arrived from Egypt. They cover the face of the earth and are threatening me. Balaam, you are a respected prophet with powerful results. I insist that you come and curse these people for me because they are too powerful. Then perhaps I will be able to conquer them and drive them from the land. I know that blessings fall on any people you bless, and curses fall on people you curse."

That night, the Lord appeared to Balaam, and warned him not to place a curse over any of these people. Indeed, *do not go with them*, tell them to go home!

The next morning Balaam said to the kings officials, "You can go home. I am not allowed to come with you."

But Balak tried again, sending more distinguished officials, and offering to pay him handsomely if he would attend and curse these people.

That night, the Lord appeared again and told him, "Since these men have come for you, you may go with them, but only do what I tell you to do."

So the next morning he got up and started off with the Moabite officials. Then he was entreated by the king to destroy the Israelites by way of a curse.

Three times King Balak persuaded Balaam to curse the children of Israel. Each time, Balaam requested that the king build him seven altars and prepare seven young bulls and seven rams for a sacrifice.

First, he met with the Lord through divination, and was told to give Balak a message: *How can I curse those whom G-d has not cursed?* So no curse was uttered, but instead he pronounced a blessing.

Second, also through divination, the Lord gave him another message, which Balaam uttered from the altars. *I have received a command to bless; G-d has blessed it and I cannot reverse it!* And further, *no curse can touch Jacob, no magic has any power against Israel!* The word of the Lord this time had become greater than the first!

Third, Balaam realised that the Lord was determined to bless Israel, so he did not resort to divination as in the first two oracles. His third oracle strengthened the position of Israel further. *He devours all the nations that oppose him, breaking their bones in pieces, shooting them with arrows. Like a lion, Israel crouches and lies down; like a lioness, who dares to arouse her? Blessed is everyone who blesses you, O Israel, and cursed is everyone who curses you.*

"BUT THE LORD HAS KEPT YOU FROM YOUR REWARD."

Balaam replied to the king, "Don't you remember what I told your messengers? I said, 'Even if Balak were to give me his palace filled with silver and gold, I would be powerless to do anything against the will of the Lord.'"

"And now, I have one final message for you, King Balak, son of Zippor. Listen to the word of the Lord, as this will come about in a time not too long from now.

"I see him, but not here and now.
I perceive him, but far in the distant future.

A star will rise from Jacob;
a sceptre will emerge from Israel.

It will crush the heads of Moab's people,
cracking the skulls of the people of Sheth."

I could hardly believe this prophecy as I pondered my own words.

Who is this star that will rise from Jacob?

Who is this sceptre that will emerge from Israel?

Advent 8:

The Shoot

Out of the stump of the line of Jesse will grow a shoot —

yes, a new Branch bearing fruit from the old root.

And the Spirit of the Lord will rest on him —

the Spirit of wisdom and understanding,

the Spirit of counsel and might,

the Spirit of knowledge and the fear of the Lord.

Isaiah 11:1–2

⌒Jesse's Story⌒

The love story between my grandparents is retold each year during Shavuot, the time of remembrance of the giving of the Law. The story tells of the area prince, Boaz, who, being about 80 years of age, fell hopelessly in love with the humble and modest Ruth, who had pledged her life to her ill-fated mother-in-law Naomi as she returned to her home country.

It's a story rooted in tragedy from both sides, as well as modesty and sacrifice.

The story starts with a man named Elimelech, who had taken his wife Naomi from Bethlehem to the land of Moab due to a drought in the area. They left the town on empty stomachs in search of a more fulfilling and worthwhile life, and despite Moab being one of Israel's contested enemies, there was no food shortages there.

During their stay in Moab, Naomi bore two sons: Mahlon and Kilion. In the course of time, Elimelech passed away and Naomi was tasked to find wives for her sons. Her primary goal was to search for worthy women from the local Moabite clans, rather than return to the land of Israel.

That's where we first meet Ruth and Orpah, though they were known by other names when they married Mahlon and Kilion.

As the story goes, both girls were great-grand daughters of King Balak, being daughters of King Eglon of Moab. That is, both Ruth and Orpah came from royal blood, who both married the sons of Naomi. These mixed race marriages did not assist the sentiment between Moab and Israel, and the fury of Balak's actions against Israel were already quite well known. Why would they want to be joined to a country that clearly wanted Israel to be cut off from the face of the earth?

Although the Law had forbidden Jewish women from marrying men from other cultures, it was not prohibited for Jewish men to marry foreign women, at the time. So Naomi's two sons married foreign women. Though they had consented to marriage, they never converted to Judaism, and the girls were not required to subscribe to Jewish laws and traditions.

Naomi felt secure when her sons married, quietly praising G-d that they would be able to carry on the name of their father after his death, so they continued to stay in the land, expecting to raise both families there. Despite their efforts, neither Ruth nor Orpah managed to conceive; they were without children, and lived with the humiliating label of barrenness among women.

If things couldn't get any worse for the family, there was further tragedy when both sons passed away. With no man to look after her or the two girls, Naomi struggled to decide whether to stay or to return to the land of her birth. She was also in a predicament: the girls had grown close to her and also shared in her grief. Shouldn't they be urged to find another husband in Moab?

Naomi had heard that good crops were available in her home town, and felt it was time to return home. With the loss of her husband and her two sons, there really was nothing left for her in the land of Moab to hold on to. Decidedly, she was determined to return alone, so she encouraged her two daughters-in-law to stay and find themselves a husband from their own clans.

Through their tears, as they were departing, Naomi named Kilion's wife Orpah (meaning *the one who kissed*) and Mahlon's wife she named Ruth (meaning *the one who clung to*). Ruth, determined to cling to Naomi, returned with her to Bethlehem as a Jewish convert, without children, and around 40 years of age. Defying her family and her culture, she cut ties with the cursed life she experienced at Moab, in the hope of a new start. Together they started off, leaving Orpah behind.

The return home to Bethlehem created quite a stir.

As a widowed elderly woman, without sons and unable to work, Naomi had no means to support herself. Further, with Ruth by her side there was a second mouth to feed. They would have to stick together just to survive, and Ruth would need to find work quickly in order to provide for her mother-in-law.

At the time of their return, Boaz had just finished burying his wife. Many people had gathered in town to mourn and grieve, as a sign of deep respect and honour for the wife of the town prince. As Naomi and Ruth entered the town on this fateful day, it seemed the entire town was surprised to see them. "Is this really Naomi?" the women asked.

"Don't call me Naomi," she responded. "Instead, call me Mara, for the Almighty has made life very bitter for me. I went away full, but the Lord has brought me home empty. Why call me Naomi when the Lord has caused me to suffer and the Almighty has sent such tragedy upon me?"

The ladies of the town did not just notice Naomi; they also looked upon Ruth, the Moabite.

My grandfather Boaz was well known in our little town of Bethlehem, having had a wife but no children to call his own. He was quite wealthy, a man of renown throughout the district. The people named him a prince.

It was time for the barley harvest, and Ruth insisted that she was going to be part of it. As she went, she happened to work in a field belonging to Boaz, not knowing that he was a close family member of Naomi.

Ruth's modesty soon became evident to all who picked in the field. She did not pick up grain like the rest and was not there to sport with the gleaners. Other younger women had come to pick up the barley as well as any other opportunities that might arise.

The fresh spring air raised emotions beyond their normally controlled limits, and the young women often flaunted with the harvesters while they worked. Word got around that they would secretly slip behind the threshing floor to fulfill the advances of the young men after the work day was completed. However not so with Ruth, who carefully ensured that she did not lead any man on with such sensual signals, or to invite harassment.

This work ethic caught the eye of Boaz.

Noticing her in the fields, Boaz asked his foreman, "Who is that woman? Who does she belong to?" The foreman replied, saying that she had been working diligently all morning behind the harvesters, and was the daughter-in-law of Naomi.

Ruth's inner beauty and sincerity struck Boaz with a deep sense of empathy and connection. That day Boaz invited her to sit with his men and eat some of the roasted grain, along with the bread and sour wine. Then he instructed his men to act kindly towards her, and not to give her a hard time.

When Ruth returned home that night, Naomi was surprised to hear of the kindness that was given by Boaz to provide for them. "May the Lord bless him!" Naomi told her daughter-in-law. "He is showing his kindness to us as well as to your dead husband. That man is one of our closest relatives, one of our family redeemers."

Then Ruth continued the story saying, "What's more, Boaz even told me to come back and stay with his harvesters until the entire harvest is completed."

"Good!" Naomi exclaimed. "Do as he says, my daughter. Stay with his young women right through the whole harvest. You might be harassed in other fields, but you'll be safe with him."

Based on her word, Ruth continued to work to the end of the barley harvest, and after that continued working with them through the wheat harvest in early summer, all the while living with her mother-in-law. Although they were both being well looked after, Naomi was concerned that her dead husband's fields and property were being neglected, and was not in a position to be able to maintain them herself. They needed to be properly managed so as to ensure the family livelihood could continue. In short, she needed to sell them to a close family member.

Word had spread throughout the area about the modest Moabite with her inherent physical beauty. She was praised like other exemplary women in the past: Sarah of Abraham and Rebekah of Isaac. Her acts of kindness to Naomi complemented her diligent work in the fields, and this did not go unnoticed with the young men. Although she had no children, this did not detract from Naomi's other possessions: the property that belonged to her husband Elimelech. Whoever was to purchase the property would also inherit the Moabite, and be expected to provide an heir for the family name through her.

Did it really matter that she was childless? Whoever secured the property was expected to continue the line of Elimelech. The new owner could only properly fulfill the role of the kinsman-redeemer to the family name by having a child through Ruth. If that did not occur then their own property could become transferred back to the family line of Elimelech in order to maintain his name in Israel, being the former descendant in the lineage.

Given that Ruth did not have children even after ten years of marriage to Mahlon, it was assumed that she was barren. Any prospective kinsman-redeemer was entering into a precarious situation that could entail the entire loss of his family livelihood if there was no heir to their estate. The notion of acquiring Ruth as part of the redemption package was not to be taken lightly.

After Boaz had supervised the harvesters, he retired to the grain pile at the end of the day. Knowing this, Naomi motioned to Ruth to show her respects to him and determine if he might be the one to redeem the property. Indeed, he had expressed his continual interest and kindness to her with grain, water and the treatment of his men towards her — but would he want to set himself in a position to redeem their land, given the risk?

Following her detailed instructions, Ruth uncovered the feet of Boaz on the threshing floor, and around midnight Boaz awoke startled that there was a woman at his feet. "Who is that?" he asked. Normally, a prince would call out curses over the frivolous actions of women who would be seeking immoral late night encounters.

"I am your servant, Ruth," she replied. "Spread the corner of your covering over me, for you are my family redeemer." This request was not simply to keep her warm while she lay beside him; this was an official yet modest invitation to determine if he had an interest in marrying her. In essence, this would ensure the longevity of the family line that Naomi wanted to protect, and gave Ruth further opportunity to demonstrate loyalty to her mother-in-law.

"The Lord bless you, my daughter!" Boaz exclaimed. "You are showing even more family loyalty now than you did before, for you have not gone after a younger man, whether rich or poor."

It was that very moment that my grand-parents knew that they were destined for each other.

They were filled with compassionate love, knowing that they were moving into an act of modesty righteousness rather than pursuing opportunistic physical pleasure. This revealed a deep appreciation and respect for each other, as well as continuing the lineage of Ruth's dead father-in-law.

Boaz, 40 years her senior, accepted the role as kinsman-redeemer in a very public ceremony at the city gate. The celebration was full of blessings upon the couple as people gathered around to take part.

The elders and all the people standing around sounded blessings upon Boaz at the announcement of their engagement.

> "We are witnesses!
> May the Lord make this woman who is
> coming into your home like Rachel and
> Leah, from whom all the nation of Israel
> descended!

May you prosper in Ephrathah
  and be famous in Bethlehem.
And may the Lord give you descendants
  by this young woman who will be like
  those of our ancestor Perez, the son of
  Tamar and Judah."

Despite the disappointing set of circumstances that had plagued them both until that time, today was cause for celebration! Boaz redeemed the field of Naomi in order to take Ruth as his bride.

When Boaz slept with his wife, the Lord enabled her to become pregnant. She who was called barren was now with child!

Then the women of the town gave Naomi deep respect and honour for what the Lord had done through Ruth.

"Praise the Lord, who has now provided a
  redeemer for your family!
May this child be famous in Israel.

May he restore your youth and care for you
  in your old age.
For he is the son of your daughter-in-law
  who loves you and has been better to you
  than seven sons!"

Naomi took the baby and cuddled him to her breast. And she cared for him as if he were her own.

The women of the town said, "Now at last Naomi has a son again!"
And they named him Obed.

The story doesn't end there.

Obed was my father, and I've just given birth to my youngest son: David.

He has seven older brothers, and some are skilled warriors who are enlisted in the king's army.

As my most favoured son, David will be a shepherd, and will look after the family sheep and goats on the hills of Ephrathah, here in Bethlehem. He will be responsible to care for the property of Elimelech, as well as the property of Boaz who also passed away.

People had rumoured carelessly about the demise of Elimelech, but the Lord has surely planted this tree steadfastly in Israel, continuing to honour the name of those who trust Him.

Given the historic and miraculous circumstances that led to their union, I pondered, "What is the significance of our family line?"

Only time will tell.

Advent 9:
The Builder

For when you die and are buried with your ancestors,

I will raise up one of your descendants,

your own offspring,

and I will make his kingdom strong.

He is the one who will build a house

—a temple—

for my name.

And I will secure his royal throne forever.

2 Samuel 7:12–13

~David's Story~

"Servant, come!"

Within seconds, my palace servant appeared with a ready ear. "My lord."

"Call Nathan for me, I have something on my heart that I want to share with him."

"Yes master," were his only words, and with a nod ran to summon the prophet.

The warmth of the sun fuelled my body as I stood on the balcony overlooking the kingdom. I was contemplating about the peace that had prevailed upon the nation, all our enemies had stopped taunting us with war and the land was at rest. For years, the Lord had fought with us to establish Israel in the Promised Land, and finally, *finally*, the blessing had become manifest.

Indeed G-d had been good to us: my throne was established and the palace was beautifully adorned with cedar panelling from Lebanon. Surely this was the height of my reign, finding acceptance from both G-d and the people. There was nothing more to be earned — we had arrived!

However grand this feeling of success was, there was one unsettled thought that I couldn't ignore: the ark of G-d was still living in a tent outside the city gates while we lived in stately buildings of our own. I had been faithful in all the Lord's house, and He was faithful to establish me as He had promised. Now that we had *arrived*, I felt that the tent of meeting was neglected — and I didn't want to treat the Lord in this way. This grieved my spirit, I was hurt that we had forgotten to look after His sanctuary.

I had leaned on the Lord since my youth, from looking after the sheep to protect them from the lion or bear; when facing off with the giant; and during these last few years where we had taken down the Lord's enemies.

The servant appeared with the prophet. "My lord, as requested..."

I turned around to meet my friend, my advisor who has stood with me through many years.

Nathan was called of G-d to the office of prophet, and I highly regarded his word as a man who spoke with sincerity and respect. There was no motive of self-promotion within him, and he stood by my side when others had deserted me.

"My friend," I was almost hesitant to bring this query, which had been on my heart for a while now, and I was unsure of how to start. So I got to the point.

"Look, I am living in a beautiful cedar palace, but the Ark of G-d is out there in a tent!"

A smile broke over the prophet's face, his heart had always synchronised with mine, and he knew the burden that lay upon me when I had consulted him in times like this. We had often discussed matters relating to the Law, and how to please G-d, drawing the same conclusions. And now he looked at me with a knowing smile of approval, giving me his blessing without hesitation.

"Go ahead and do whatever you have in mind, for the Lord is with you." His words were sincere and trustworthy. I knew that my soul would find encouragement in consulting with him.

"Thank you, my friend." That night I could not sleep due to my own levels of excitement and satisfaction that the new project was going to bring. Not that this was to be self-serving, as my heart's desire has always been to see the glory of G-d manifested amongst us. As my father and grandfather had taught me, those who seek to honour the Lord walk in the realm of His blessing, and the Lord honours those whom He loves.

But that night, Nathan had a different experience from the Lord. The Lord came and spoke directly.

> "Go and tell my servant David, 'This is what the Lord has declared: Are you the one to build a house for me to live in? I have never lived in a house, from the day I brought the Israelites out of Egypt until this very day. I have always moved from one place to another with a tent and a Tabernacle as my dwelling.
>
> Yet no matter where I have gone with the Israelites, I have never once complained to Israel's tribal leaders, the shepherds of my people Israel. I have never asked them, "Why haven't you built Me a beautiful cedar house?"'"

Taken aback, Nathan realised that his words were not from the Lord, but had come from the personal and spiritual alignment from his friendship with the king. His heart grieved at the assumption, apologising to the Lord for speaking without approaching Him about it first.

The Lord smiled, and assured him that it was good to have this thought for the tabernacle, but David was not to be the one to build the house, but someone further down his lineage.

The Lord recommenced, saying, "Now go and say to my servant David:

> "This is what the Lord of Heaven's Armies has declared: I took you from tending sheep in the pasture and selected you to be the leader of my people Israel.
>
> I have been with you wherever you have gone, and I have destroyed all your enemies before your eyes. Now I will make your name as famous as anyone who has ever lived on the earth!
>
> And I will provide a homeland for my people Israel, planting them in a secure place where they will never be disturbed.
>
> Evil nations won't oppress them as they've done in the past, starting from the time I appointed judges to rule my people Israel. And I will give you rest from all your enemies.

Furthermore, the Lord declares that he will make a house for you—a dynasty of kings!

For when you die and are buried with your ancestors, I will raise up one of your descendants, your own offspring, and I will make his kingdom strong.

He is the one who will build a house—a temple—for my name. And I will secure his royal throne forever.

I will be his father, and he will be my son. If he sins, I will correct and discipline him with the rod, like any father would do.

But my favour will not be taken from him as I took it from Saul, whom I removed from your sight.

Your house and your kingdom will continue before me for all time, and your throne will be secure forever."

The next morning Nathan brought in the word from the Lord, and shared it just as it had been given to him. My dreams and hopes of building a house for the Lord had been challenged, though in a good way.

I needed time to sit and pray, and reflect upon this word of prophecy. My heart swelled with a radiance consisting of humility, gratitude and honour. What I had planned and hoped to do for the Lord seemed to be given back to me with greater and longer lasting promises.

I spread out my hands before the Lord, and prayed.

> "Who am I, O Sovereign Lord, and what is my family, that you have brought me this far?
>
> And now, Sovereign Lord, in addition to everything else, you speak of giving your servant a lasting dynasty!
>
> Do you deal with everyone this way, O Sovereign Lord?"

Surely G-d rewards those who earnestly seek Him, who hold fast to His name.

> "What more can I say to you? You know what your servant is really like, Sovereign Lord.
>
> Because of your promise and according to your will, you have done all these great things and have made them known to your servant.
>
> How great you are, O Sovereign Lord! There is no one like you. We have never even heard of another G-d like you!

What other nation on earth is like your
people Israel? What other nation, O G-d,
have you redeemed from slavery to be your
own people?

You made a great name for yourself when
you redeemed your people from Egypt. You
performed awesome miracles and drove
out the nations and gods that stood in their
way. You made Israel your very own people
forever, and you, O Lord, became their G-d."

"And now, O Lord G-d, I am your servant;
do as you have promised concerning me
and my family. Confirm it as a promise that
will last forever. And may your name be
honoured forever so that everyone will say,
'The Lord of Heaven's Armies is G-d over
Israel!' And may the house of your servant
David continue before you forever.

"O Lord of Heaven's Armies, G-d of Israel,
I have been bold enough to pray this prayer
to you because you have revealed all this to
your servant, saying, 'I will build a house for
you—a dynasty of kings!'

For you are G-d, O Sovereign Lord. Your
words are truth, and you have promised these
good things to your servant. And now, may it

please you to bless the house of your servant,
so that it may continue forever before you.
For you have spoken, and when you grant a
blessing to your servant, O Sovereign Lord, it
is an eternal blessing!"

Towards the end of the day, as I again rested
on the balcony in the cool of the afternoon,
overlooking the vastness of the kingdom that the
Lord had clearly established, I could only wonder
who was going to receive this blessing.

I was content to learn that it was not for me to
build a house for the Lord, but that G-d was
going to build an everlasting house for me,
instead.

These words kept turning through my head until
I finally fell asleep.

*I will raise up one of your descendants, your own offspring,
and I will make his kingdom strong.*

*He is the one who will build a house—a temple—for
my name.*

And I will secure his royal throne forever.

Advent 10:
The Virgin

All right then,

the Lord himself will give you the sign.

Look! The virgin will conceive a child!

She will give birth to a son

and will call him Emmanuel

(which means 'G-d is with us').

Luke 23:32–34a

Isaiah's Story

Standing before the great white throne, the heavenly presence saturated my entire being, the holiness of G-d surrounded me and a weight of glory rested on me. There were creatures around the throne that attended to the Eternal Being, crying out "Holy, holy, holy is the Lord of Heaven's Armies! The whole earth is filled with His glory!"

While they spoke, the foundations of the Temple shook, and the entire building filled with smoke — the incense of heaven. As if in an earth-quake, the shaking of this heavenly temple caused me to quake in terror with the feeling of impending doom.

This was not merely a place of worship, but the centre of command where battle instructions were issued and directions were given to the angelic hosts that carried them onto the earthly plain.

This was a holy battle ground!
The Temple was the centre of heaven!

As this episode unfolded, I became entirely self-conscious of my own sinfulness, my own lack of holiness. The enveloping holiness of G-d contrasted against my own worthlessness. I was unworthy to stand in this majestic Presence, and cried out, "Woe to me! I am such a sinful man. My lips are filthy. I live among people with filthy lips. Everything we say and speak is disgusting!" Even though we were chosen as His special possession, it was obvious that our nation has no respect for the holiness of G-d, nor desire to follow His ways.

As I confessed my sins before the throne, one of the seraphim flew to me with a burning coal he had taken from the altar with a pair of tongs. He touched my lips with it and said, "See, this coal has touched your lips. Now your guilt is removed, and your sins are forgiven."

Freedom.

FREEDOM.

A weight of guilt lifted from my being, and the heaviness departed leaving me floating in light.

F R E E D O M.

I was breathing as if for the first time, drawing strength from the atmosphere of heaven.

Years later I was serving the Lord and performing my duties as prophet to the king of Judah.

King Ahaz was just twenty years old when he ascended the throne of Judah under Davids royal line, after his father Jotham passed away. Although his father loved the Lord, Jotham had refused to destroy the pagan shrines and as a result the people offered sacrifices and burned incense in those places - instead of the Temple of the Lord. When Ahaz inherited the reign, he took a deeper interest in foreign gods by offering sacrifices and burning incense at the pagan shrines and on the hills and under every green tree. Naturally this infuriated the Lord who brought Israel out of the land of Egypt.

During his early reign, the king of Israel and the king of Aram (Syria) joined forces to attack Judah. This caused the hearts of the people and King Ahaz of Judah to melt with fear. The brothers of Jacob were fighting against each other, and even resorted to gaining outside help!

The Lord sent me with a message to Ahaz, saying:

"Tell him to stop worrying.
Tell him he doesn't need to fear the fierce
anger of those two burned-out embers,
King Rezin of Syria and Pekah son of
Remaliah of Israel.

Yes, the kings of Syria and Israel are plotting
against him, but this is what the Sovereign
Lord says:

'This invasion will never happen; it will
never take place.'"

Despite this strong word of encouragement, Ahaz
disregarded this word from the Lord and sought
the favour of another king in the north to assist
with the battle, King Tiglath-pileser of Assyria.

Ahaz sent him this message. "I am your servant
and your vassal. Come up and rescue me from
the attacking armies of Aram and Israel." Then
Ahaz took the silver and gold from the Temple
of the Lord and the palace treasury and sent
it as payment to the Assyrian king. So the king
of Assyria aligned with the king of Judah and
attacked the Aramean capital of Damascus and
led its population away as captives, resettling them
in Kir. He also killed King Rezin.

King Ahaz then went to Damascus to meet with King Tiglath-pileser of Assyria. While he was there, he took special note of the altar. Then he sent a model of the altar to Uriah the priest, along with its design in full detail. Uriah followed the king's instructions and built an altar just like it, and it was ready before the king returned from Damascus.

Although Israel had planned an attack against Judah, it never eventuated. The kings of Syria and Israel were defeated as a result of the mutual treaty that king Ahaz had set up with the king of Assyria.

As a result, Ahaz embraced the sacrificial system of worship, and replaced Jewish tradition and culture.

Ahaz instructed Uriah about the use of the new altar in Jerusalem.

> "Use the new altar for the morning sacrifices of burnt offering, the evening grain offering, the king's burnt offering and grain offering, and the burnt offerings of all the people, as well as their grain offerings and liquid offerings.
>
> Sprinkle the blood from all the burnt offerings and sacrifices on the new altar. The bronze altar will be for my personal use only."

The king removed the bronze altar from its place in front of the Lord's Temple and had it installed on the north side of the new altar which stood where the bronze altar was set up. On this new altar, fashioned after the practises of the foreign gods, Ahaz offered his son as a burnt offering to Molech.

Ahaz found an interest in the technology of the Assyrians and sought to implement them into the palace at Jerusalem. After one visit, Ahaz returned with a stepped sundial, which enabled him to consistently predict the time of day. As the sun rose in the east, the shadow of the sun rose on the eastern side steps, and after midday the shadow rose up the western side steps. Although this was initially a portable model, Ahaz incorporated this shadow clock function into the steps of the Kings Palace which enabled the sun's shadow to ascend the slope from the King's Palace eastward down to the Horse Gate (in the city wall) and ascend the other set of stairs from the Horse Gate up to the south side of the Temple.

Admiring the king of Assyria, Ahaz removed the canopy that had been constructed inside the palace for use on the Sabbath day, as well as the king's outer entrance to the Temple of the Lord. This continued the trend of disregarding the established laws and statutes, creating further separation between Ahaz and the Lord.

Ahaz's stubborn heart seemed to have no intention to follow the ways of the Lord, and he instead replaced everything that was considered godly with those of foreign gods. His treaty and alignment with the King of Assyria provided him comfort against the surrounding nations, but it broke the long-established covenant that G-d had with Abraham and his descendants.

It was sometime later that the Lord sent me with this message to king Ahaz.

"Ask the Lord for a sign, Ahaz. Make it as difficult as you want, as high as heaven or as deep as the place of the dead."

But the king refused. "No," he said, "I will not test the Lord like that."

Clearly his intention was not to engage with the Lord, even when invited. G-d was clearly wanting to determine if there was any room left in Ahaz's heart for Himself, and was willing to prove it to the king without reservation.

But this wasn't enough, and Ahaz's clear refusal to respond or co-operate infused a holy anger within me, and I charged him:

"Listen well, you royal family of David! Isn't it enough to exhaust human patience? Must you exhaust the patience of my G-d as well? All right then, the Lord himself will give you the sign:

Look! The virgin will conceive a child!

She will give birth to a son and will call him Emmanuel (which means 'G-d is with us').

By the time this child is old enough to choose what is right and reject what is wrong, he will be eating yogurt and honey.

For before the child is that old, the lands of the two kings you fear so much will both be deserted.

Then the Lord will bring things on you, your nation, and your family unlike anything since Israel broke away from Judah.

He will also bring the king of Assyria upon you!"

The king's heart collapsed.

All his hopes relied on friendly allegiance with the king of Assyria: replacing the altar of burnt offering with that of the northern ally; burning incense on the hills and under every green tree; trading the valuable items of worship for a replica made in the image of pagan gods, and embracing their practises.

Who is this virgin that will bring forth a son?

And who is this Emmanual that will be 'G-d with us'?

Will there be a chance to bring us back to repentance to experience the holiness of G-d?

Advent 11:
The Angel Gabriel

In the sixth month of Elizabeth's pregnancy,

G-d sent the angel Gabriel to Nazareth,

a village in Galilee, to a virgin named Mary.

She was engaged to be married to a man named Joseph,

a descendant of King David.

Gabriel appeared to her and said,

'Greetings, favoured woman!

The Lord is with you!

Luke 1:26–28

Gabriel's Story

The usual lively atmosphere hushed in silence as arrays of angels anticipated that Father G-d was about to speak. As if in unison, all faces turned towards the throne to hear the message that was about to be shared by the Majestic voice of heaven.

"Gabriel, come." The request was not just an instruction but an invitation. Visible light flickered as though a strong candle throughout the realm of heaven as He spoke, lighting up the atmosphere. The sound of His voice drew my full attention to Father's words, eager to hear what would be shared.

We had been together since the beginning of time eternal, where I was appointed as the angel to serve and minister to the Son. This role meant that I was always to be by the side of the Manifest Glory of heaven — it was both a delight and a weighty responsibility, one that I did not take lightly. The pleasure of attending to the Most High resonated throughout my being, it was not so much duty as it was a love-filled relationship based around personal sacrifice.

"Gabriel, we have another assignment for you."

I smiled, thinking of the last time I was appointed to leave the presence of heaven in order to attend to a man on the earthly realm. Previously, Daniel the prophet was praying at the time of the evening sacrifice and I was given the command to provide insight and understanding of the vision that he had received from heaven.

Daniel had been interceding on behalf of the people of Israel, confessing their sins and disobedience, acknowledging that they had refused to listen to the voice of G-d, and pleaded for forgiveness and mercy on their behalf that G-d could act without delay. At that time I was sent swiftly to explain the message, and to put in perspective the things that were to come upon the world. The interpretation of the vision made Daniel sick for many days, as it pertained to the times at the end.

Father continued. "Your first assignment is to respond to the prayers of a priest. One has been selected to offer incense in the Temple, and has prayed asking for a child for his barren wife. You can share that his prayer will be answered and that his wife Elizabeth will give him a son. He is to name him John."

The message itself seemed quite simple, and I was searching the intent of Father's heart to determine why this required the Lords angel to deliver it. Father knew my concern and responded to my thoughts, saying that this was not an ordinary child. He would prepare the way for the Christ-child.

"Tell the priest that he will have great joy and gladness, and many will rejoice at the birth of his son, for he will be great in the eyes of the Lord. The boy must never touch wine or other alcoholic drinks. He will be filled with the Holy Spirit, even before his birth."

I almost protested about the Holy Spirit being given at birth, as this was something that has never been granted since the days of Adam. However I knew that Father has His ways and understood that this was part of an eternal plan; I was simply His messenger. The boy would grow into a man that led a specific purpose in life, and his birth would be miraculous because his parents were well past the age of child bearing. He would be a child of promise, just like Samuel the son of Hannah, Isaac the son of Sarah, Joseph the son of Rachel and Jacob the son of Rebecca.

"Finally, tell him that when the boy grows up he will turn many Israelites to the Lord their G-d. He will be a man with the spirit and power of Elijah. He will prepare the people for the coming of the Lord. He will turn the hearts of the fathers to their children, and he will cause those who are rebellious to accept the wisdom of the godly."

The simple command now contained a large volume of messages to be shared with the priest. This was to be no ordinary child, and the gravity of the assignment swelled within my chest as it became clear now that the Lord had a larger plan in hand, this was not just a one-off assignment.

Again, knowing my thoughts, Father shared the rest of the plan that had been hidden from the created order.

"After this, I have a second assignment for you." Heaven glowed once again with the power of His voice shining throughout the atmosphere. I had a greater anticipation of what was to come after this first assignment, though it was likewise hidden from my understanding.

I pressed in closer, excited to hear that heaven and earth were coming together again, just as in the beginning. Father expected His plans to be executed swiftly so as to manifest His intentions with minimum delay and disruptions.

He continued. "Six months from now, I will send you to a young woman. Unlike Elizabeth, she is a virgin."

I was puzzled as to the assignment, there was something missing from Fathers instructions that did not present this situation as anything significant. And yet I knew that the task I was being instructed about wouldn't be miniscule. So I bowed my head gently towards the Son, waiting for further instructions.

"Her name is Mary, and her parents devoted her for service in the temple from a young age. Mary has proven herself as a humble servant in all my house, and I trust her with this task."

My curiosity piqued, the message was still hidden. Father has never shown a lack of transparency when providing assignments like this, however in this case it was long in coming. I was about to find out why.

"Gabriel, I am sending the Son to take the form of a servant. He will be the fullness of the godhead in bodily form, and will be incarnate. He will live on earth, just as the first Adam did."

As the Lord's personal body guard and assistant, I was not aware of these plans. How could they have hidden this for so long? I turned to the Son, and asked, "Are you willing to do this?"

With a loving smile he confirmed, "Yes, I am." I felt the power of His presence provide me with physical strength; His words refreshed and calmed me.

There was something more to this situation that I could not yet understand, but I knew the Lord would not create disorder. Before I could probe further, the Lord Himself continued the explanation.

"Gabriel, I will enter the human race being born as a baby — but not by human conception. The Holy Spirit will overshadow Mary and she will conceive. As a man born of woman, I must maintain the holiness and purity of God; so the baby born to her must not inherit the sin-stained DNA of Adam."

The storyline started to piece itself together, but it was still a mystery. If I was to tell her that she was going to get pregnant by the Holy Spirit, what effect would that have on her life? And the life of the One that I was assigned to?

Father answered my question, confirming my thoughts and provided the context for what was follow.

"Gabriel, Mary has found favour with G-d through her humility and eagerness to know Me. I am giving her the responsibility to carry the Christ-child, and with Joseph they will raise him as their own. They are to give Him the name 'Jesus'."

The message was weighty, not because it was my duty to undertake it on behalf of the Lord, but because of what it meant to the armies of heaven. Without the Son in heaven, the throne was open to any entity that may want to approach Father G-d with accusations against men with no-one to defend them.

Father continued. "Jesus will be very great and He will be called the Son of the Most High. The Lord G-d will give him the throne of his ancestor

David. And he will reign over Israel forever. His Kingdom will never end!"

I had but one question that demanded an answer before I took this assignment: Would Mary agree to this plan?

The Father looked at the Son, and together they turned to me in unison to answer my thoughts.

"Mary is our humble vessel. She knows that her life purpose is greater than simply marrying Joseph. She is pleased to be the servant of the Lord, and we know that she will agree to this proposal."

With this statement of conficence, I was ready. "Ok, I'll go."

Advent 12:
The Unbelieving Priest

While Zechariah was in the sanctuary,

an angel of the Lord appeared to him,

standing to the right of the incense altar.

Zechariah was shaken and overwhelmed with fear

when he saw him.

But the angel said,

"Don't be afraid, Zechariah!

G-d has heard your prayer.

Your wife, Elizabeth, will give you a son,

and you are to name him John.

He will be a man with the spirit and power of Elijah.

He will prepare the people for the coming of the Lord.

He will turn the hearts of the fathers to their children,

and he will cause those who are rebellious
to accept the wisdom of the godly."

Luke 1:11–13,17

⁓Zechariah's Story⁓

"I really am grateful that I wasn't struck dead, Elizabeth."

We were discussing the time of my visit to the sanctuary, that *once in a lifetime event* where I was chosen by lot, to burn incense at the altar before the Lord.

My priestly division was one of twenty-four families, each of which had three hundred priests. So to receive the honour of being selected meant that you had to be one of the very few chosen ones to whom the lot would fall. And in this case, it fell to me — something completely unexpected — and yet, the Lord answered my prayer in a way that I couldn't have imagined.

Recalling this to my wife, "Remember, love, those years where we pined for a child. We followed the righteous requirements of the Law, and yet heaven was silent. We hoped, begged and prayed that G-d would give us a family — a son or a daughter — and yet despite this, we bore no children."

Elizabeth blushed, tired to have to think of it again; her frail hands swaddling the miracle baby boy that was an answer to their prayers. Baby John waved his arms in a rattle, not aware of the depth of tearful emotion that was going on around him, and let out a pant.

I found it hard to swallow the thought of what we had been through together. We were now well into our sixties; our lives had seemed to have wasted away; and G-d had been silent for far too long.

I recalled our wedding day, both of us being of the line of Aaron, where we were expecting the dew of heaven to bring forth the priestly blessing upon our home. "Surely, our family will extend throughout the region, we have the fullness of G-d upon us!" Such was our cry at the time. We were full of excitement, knowing that the next generation would continue the requirements of the priestly duties through the children that we would bring forth.

That was then … many years ago. But over time, our hopes faded. And as the years passed, our expectations turned to anxiety. We felt the pain of heaven's silence was all too real, with our bodies aged to the point where we knew we could no longer expect to have a child. There was no word from heaven, no enlightenment, no child that we could call our own.

Ultimately, our desperation turned to anger. How long did I have to be obedient to my calling, being faithful, and demonstrating righteousness, before G-d would hear?

"No! It wasn't fair!" I blurted.

My memory of these events escaped through the thoughts held captive in my mind, spilling out of my mouth. I hadn't intended to speak, and had startled my wife with my abrupt line of war.

"Sorry, dear, I didn't mean for that to come out. It's just that when I recall the injustice of being left behind, anger rises within me. The Lord could have acted sooner, if it were to be fair."

She turned to me, and held the baby up so I could nurse him. He had such an adorable sweet-smelling baby face, distracting my futility for a while with his cuteness.

But it wasn't only me that felt this way, our nation was restless. It was four hundred years since G-d last spoke to us. Four hundred years! As a nation, and from the priesthood, we had been waiting for the next big move of G-d, waiting to see His power move like He did in Egypt and overthrew Pharaoh. We yearned for even a candle to be lit that would give us hope and comfort that would soothe our national pain, under the tyrannical and illegitimate ruler called Herod.

From the prophet Malachi, G-d's last words to us were:

> "Look, I am sending you the prophet Elijah
>   before the great and dreadful day
>   of the Lord arrives.
>
> He will turn the hearts of the fathers
>   to their children,
> and the hearts of children to their fathers.
>
> Otherwise I will come and strike the land
>   with a curse."

It's been four hundred years!
Where is this promised Elijah?
We have been waiting, Lord, and you have done nothing.

NOTHING!

As the lot was cast for me that day, my posture was not one of gratitude or thankfulness; instead my heart was raging against the lack of words from the Lord, the lack of answers to prayer. There was no doubt in my mind that G-d had abandoned His children.

"Zechariah, you're up!"

The faces of the priests almost reflected the disbelief of my own heart when the lot fell to me. Not that they were jealous, but they had learnt from my actions and were observing my attitude which revealed that G-d chooses even those *who are not in a good place with Him* to be welcomed into the sanctuary.

"I recalled entering the sanctuary, and when I lit the incense an angel appeared. His presence was frightening; I was not prepared in my heart to have such an encounter with G-d at this time."

Elizabeth looked up, recounting the fear in my face as I retold the story once again. "Yes I think I would have felt the same way, if I was allowed to burn incense on the altar." she assured.

"And then the angel said, 'Zechariah! G-d has heard your prayer. Your wife, Elizabeth, will give you a son, and you are to name him John.' Well that didn't make sense! I immediately felt that I needed to correct him, as there is no one in our family that has the name of John. The baby was to be named after myself, Zechariah."

A quizzical smile crept along the face of my wife, and I realised that she had noticed that stubborn streak in me at other times, and had just not mentioned it. This time I knew that I had overstepped the mark, as it had become clear that the angel didn't want me to interrupt his message.

"The angel continued, saying, 'You will have great joy and gladness, and many will rejoice at his birth, for he will be great in the eyes of the Lord. He must never touch wine or other alcoholic drinks. He will be filled with the Holy Spirit, even before his birth. And he will turn many Israelites to the Lord their G-d.'"

When he told me this, I knew that our son would be required to follow the Nazarite Laws. In all honesty, I felt this word from the angel was overbearing, as this is not something that he was given a choice in — he wasn't even born yet! I feared that he may go the way of Samson, who died because he ignored the calling on his life.

"And then he said something that made me stop. Surely the Lord was now playing some kind of trick on us? He said, 'He will be a man with the spirit and power of Elijah. He will prepare the people for the coming of the Lord. He will turn the hearts of the fathers to their children, and he will cause those who are rebellious to accept the wisdom of the godly.'"

"That is, our son will be a man with the spirit and power of Elijah. Is G-d really saying that this is the promised Elijah from of old? Of all the people, and our bodies are as good as dead, this would now usher in the great and dreadful day of the Lord?"

My cynicism had hit an all-time high. The angel could say almost anything at this point in time and it would not change the fact that G-d had deserted us throughout our lifetime, and had deserted Israel for four hundred years. These undeniable facts caused me to stand my ground, my heart as stone. I was cynical.

"So I answered the angel, 'How can I be sure this will happen? I'm an old man now, and my wife is also well along in years.' Didn't he realise that his words were merely a slap in the face, that G-d didn't answer our prayers when we needed it the most? I was angry because we have been the ridicule of our clans for so long, despite our hopes and prayers, and yet there was no answer from heaven. I really felt that G-d did not care for us, as much as we were obedient to Him and His Laws."

My wife could feel the cold words flowing freely from my lips, but it didn't disturb her peace or the semblance of hope that she now held in her arms. Stopping myself, I gazed towards my loving wife, bringing my mind back to the present, and connected once again to this wonderful woman who had come to rest in the joy of the Lord.

My heart softened, and I stopped talking, allowing the goodness of the fulfilment of G-d's promises to rest in front of my eyes for a while. A faint childish cry came from the baby, which tugged at my heart strings even further. Yes, here is what the angel promised, held firmly in our arms, the start of our family together. And yes, at this present point in time, I am very grateful.

"And then that's when it happened!" I recommenced the story, shocking myself into the reality of what I had just come through for the last nine months. The thoughts of my heart had been revealed to the heavenly visitor, I wasn't just angry at what G-d had done, or rather, had not done; I didn't want to accept the words of the angel at all. I didn't care what he was saying, whether it would be blessing or curse. But for me, for us, in our situation, where G-d remained silent all our lives, I wasn't prepared to pretend to be grateful just because G-d felt it was His time to take action."

I needed to take a deep breath, as I felt myself getting wound up again, and I didn't want to break the solemnity of the moment with my own levels of aggravation.

"Then the angel said, 'I am Gabriel! I stand in the very presence of G-d. It was he who sent me to bring you this good news! But now, since you didn't believe what I said, you will be silent and unable to speak until the child is born. For my words will certainly be fulfilled at the proper time.'"

"Well, I felt somewhat embarrassed, to say the least. When I came out of the sanctuary, I could not speak. Everyone was asking me questions, and all I could do was some simple gestures to let them know that I had seen an angel. They figured it out soon enough, but didn't understand why I couldn't speak."

I kneeled over to take up the child, our son, into my own arms; to hold the goodness of G-d who gave me that word from an angel, and who chose not to strike me down for my unbelief.

"Just who are you going to become, my son, my son of promise?"

Closing my eyes, and holding John closely to my chest, I breathed these words of life into the boy.

"And you, my little son,
will be called the prophet of the Most High,
because you will prepare the way for the Lord.

You will tell his people how to find salvation
through forgiveness of their sins.

Because of God's tender mercy,
the morning light from heaven is about
to break upon us,
to give light to those who sit in darkness
and in the shadow of death,
and to guide us to the path of peace."

Is it any coincidence that my name means *the Lord has remembered*?

The Lord has surely remembered, and is preparing the way of salvation.

Advent 13:
The Lord's Servant

Mary asked the angel,

"But how can this happen?

I am a virgin."

The angel replied,

"The Holy Spirit will come upon you,

and the power of the Most High will overshadow you.

So the baby to be born will be holy, and he will be called

the Son of G-d."

Mary responded,

"I am the Lord's servant.

May everything you have said about me come true."
And then the angel left her.

Luke 1:34–35,38

⌁Mary's Story⌁

The priests knew me as the Temple girl. I grew up in our nations centre of worship from a young age, as my parents had offered me up as service to the Lord as an answer to their prayers. Each morning I helped prepare the setting for the early sacrifices, which included cleaning the offering utensils, sweeping the floor and keeping an eye on what was to be prepared as people came in to worship.

Throughout the day I assisted the priests, scribes and others to fulfill their duties. My presence in the Temple created a softness in the air and the leaders smiled as they saw how diligent I was at my duties.

I knew no other life, unlike other kids that grew up outside the Temple. I felt that my parents had made a wise decision, and I was content within myself to be here. I was affectionately called 'The servant of the Lord' as I prepared myself for a lifetime of service, in line with what I felt was my calling.

I was genuinely happy to be so richly involved and integrated into the restoration of our nation. Once again it seemed that G-d had found favour with us, the children of Abraham; that He had remembered His promises and was restoring our land. We knew that our time in captivity had ended, and were awaiting the arrival of the Messiah — a topic frequently discussed among the leaders, as they had hoped that one of them would receive the heavenly appointment by angelic visitation.

Six months ago we thought this was to be the case. My uncle Zechariah, of the priestly clan, was chosen by lot to offer the incense prayer, and encountered a powerful interaction with an angel. We knew something was happening at the time because the incense offering doesn't usually last more than a few minutes, and his time in there was lengthy. *A temple girl notices these things.*

When he came out, he couldn't speak, but we knew from his actions that he had an encounter, and we wondered if this meant that he was to be the Chosen one, the Deliverer of Israel. But this wasn't to be the case, it seemed, and he returned home.

This event created a stir among the priests, because if G-d was starting to talk with His people again after the long silence then this meant that the Temple would have to be made ready. And it was surrounding this that they discussed me and my situation. It had become apparent that very soon I would be of age that would make the Temple unclean. Until now, at least, I was able to perform my duties and assist the running of the Temple without any cause for alarm. However they recognised that as I approached my teenage years that I would need to leave.

After much discussion, instead of sending me back to my parents, and having made enquiries, they were granted permission to seek for me a husband so that I could marry. This wasn't taken lightly, as they knew the calling on my life was complemented with my sincerity and eagerness to ensure that the things of G-d were handled the right way.

Through the temple tradition, the eligible young men were brought forward but none were found suitable until an older man, Joseph, had been selected. With his wife they had had two children, but since she had passed away, he was called by the priests to test the budding of Aaron's staff for marriage.

As it so happened, the rod budded — in line with the prophecy — and we were betrothed. Together, we left for Galilee, where Joseph's brother Clopas and family lived. This is where we would stay until the time of our wedding day.

It was here, during my time of waiting and preparation, after I had been released from my temple service and before I was to be joined to my husband, that the angel appeared in my early morning prayers.

This glistening heavenly brightness shone all around, lighting up my room with a glow that penetrated into my soft skin and radiated my face. I was not accustomed to visions or apparitions, despite being in service at the temple for around ten years.

"Rejoice! Woman of favour! The Lord is with you!"

His voice was majestic and authoritative, filled with the sound of deep strings spoken as if from the realms of eternity. The force of his breath pushed my hair back and I was left confused and disturbed as to what this all might mean.

My face flushed red as I soaked in his words, as this greeting seemed to be out of place for such a girl as me.

The angel continued, saying, "Don't be afraid, Mary, for you have found favour with G-d!"

When he said this, my spirit revived with the thought that my dedication to the Lord had been noticed. These years of service in the temple were not going to be wasted, as the assuring words penetrated deep into my heart. A heavenly peace settled upon me.

At this, I was going to thank the angel for his unexpected appearance and to bid him farewell when he raised his hand to motion me to silence.

"Mary, the Lord has seen your lowly state and has a calling for you, outside the temple."

The angel might not have been aware that I was about to be married, and from then on I would be honouring and serving my husband, instead of being devoted completely to the Lord — as has been my time until now. I sensed that there was a bigger picture being drawn, and I bowed my head to hear what was about to be said. His penetrating eyes captured my full attention, this was a moment of seriousness.

"Mary, you will conceive and give birth to a son, and you will name him Jesus."

He paused, waiting for me to process what had been spoken. My mind raced for answers as to how this might occur so I asked, "How can this happen, for I have not known a man?"

The angel knew that my question was not borne in unbelief but more out of sincere curiosity; however he did not answer me straight away.

"Mary, this child will be very great and will be called the Son of the Most High."

How can this be a great child, when I am just a servant girl? I have spent my entire life in the Temple, and now about to be married because I was no longer useful in the service of the Lord. The angel responded to my thoughts as though I had spoken them out loud, showing me that my situation was to fulfil the promises of G-d to Israel.

"Mary, the Lord G-d will give Him the throne of His ancestor David."

The prophecy of Nathan was well known: that long after King David had passed away, the Lord promised that a ruler would sit on David's throne forever, where it was said, 'Your house and your kingdom will continue before Me forever.' *This was to be no ordinary child. This was the answer that Israel had longed for!*

"Mary, He will reign over Israel forever; His Kingdom will never end!"

I was still puzzled as to how the angel could read my thoughts as I contemplated the thread of our conversation. The extent of the angel's words spoken over me right now was enormous. This was nothing less than the fulfillment of the promises to Abraham, Isaac and Jacob; this was the coming Messiah!

"But sir," I interrupted the angel to ask, "How will this be since I am a virgin?" In my heart I had accepted the divine appointment but did not understand how this would come about, the message was still not clear.

The angel grimaced at my question, and I sensed the answer immediately in my spirit through the words of Isaiah the prophet, The Lord himself will give you the sign. *Look! The virgin will conceive a child! She will give birth to a son and will call him Emmanuel.*

I stopped myself, and reconsidered the thought that had come from the angel, *The virgin will conceive a child.*

That's me. Wait — is that right? Is that scripture pointing to me? Am I really the fulfillment of this word? I didn't need the angel to respond, the truth of the question became fully known. Now I could see why he was sent to bring me this message. This was the fulfillment of the promises and the breaking of the new dawn.

The angel replied, "The Holy Spirit will come upon you, and the power of the Most High will overshadow you. So the baby to be born will be holy, and he will be called the Son of G-d."

My heart warmed at his words, and I closed my eyes to allow myself to take in all the energy of the moment that we were in. And with that, Gabriel touched my shoulder to release a beautiful holy and heavenly peace over my body.

The presence of the Holy Spirit was tangible, covering me from the top of my head down to the tips of my toes. This was a holy calling, a divine appointment, the start of a new life of service to the Lord.

The angel continued. "What's more, your relative Elizabeth has become pregnant in her old age! People used to say she was barren, but she has conceived a son and is now in her sixth month. For the word of G-d will never fail."

This seemed to be a second message that the angel was delivering, a second set of scriptures were being fulfilled, promised by the prophet Malachi. *I am sending you the prophet Elijah before the great and dreadful day of the Lord arrives.*

I needed to run and see what was happening to Elizabeth. Was this related to the angelic visitation that Zechariah had six months ago in the temple? Did the Lord promise a child to them as well? I knew they longed for a family and had felt they had been overlooked, but continued to be faithful in all the Lords house and to praise G-d for all His goodness towards them, and the house of Israel.

My heart settled, and I allowed my eyes to rest back onto the face of the angel. His majestic appearance was both reassuring and frightening, and I drew comfort from his words that provided support and direction. This was a holy ordination.

How else could I respond?

"I am the Lord's servant."

As I spoke the angel appeared to welcome my words, and together a form of covenant had commenced.

"May everything you have said about me come true."

And with that, the angel left.

Advent 14:
The Pregnant Cousin

Elizabeth gave a glad cry
and exclaimed to Mary,

"God has blessed you above all women,
and your child is blessed.

Why am I so honoured,
that the mother of my Lord should visit me?
When I heard your greeting,
the baby in my womb jumped for joy.

You are blessed because you believed
that the Lord would do what he said."

Luke 1:42–45

⁓Elizabeth's Story⁓

All my life, it seems, I had been forgotten.

Growing up in the hill country of Judea, betrothed from my youth as was Jewish custom, I longed for my own family. Our heritage was of the direct priestly line of Aaron, and we revelled in fervent expectation that we would see good things to come.

Our father Abraham had been promised the sacred covenant — which had been sworn with an oath — that G-d would rescue us from our enemies so we can serve Him without fear, in holiness and righteousness for as long as we would live. And we had. My husband Zechariah was a respected man in our community and carried out the duties of a priest with diligence and care on behalf of the house of Israel.

We were careful to obey the law, and go beyond
that to care for the poor and needy when we
had opportunity. We were faithful in all that
G-d had called us to do. And yet those days
where we expected blessing — as a result of our
faithfulness — had faded into an abandoned
silence. The opportunity for having children was
now lost in time.

I was lonely.

The loneliness set in during our middle age years,
when all our friends were blessed with children
that would bring them joy and life. But without
child, I often wondered if this was part of an
unresolved curse? How could anyone look at us
and see the blessing of the Lord on our lives?
For years we had lived with the expectation of a
son or a daughter, and yet opportunity seemed to
have abandoned us this time. We were counting
the years.

Fifty years.

Emotionally bereft, I closed my eyes each time
these memories surfaced. The sadness left my
heart aching, testing my faithfulness to G-d. I am
grateful, though, for the times that we had been
able to live together until then.

Nonetheless, it wasn't easy to hide the feeling that we had been overlooked.

Forgotten.

I wiped a tear away from my eyes, restraining my sadness and looked down upon my enlarged belly. The vision in the temple totally changed things. Indeed, G-d had heard our prayer, and was ready to answer it. My husband and I had longed and prayed for children over many years, but until then heaven was silent.

He, too, had felt the pain of this unresolved dream. Did G-d really have the power to answer prayer? Was G-d really looking after us all this time? It was hard not to be cynical, especially when we had proven our faithfulness for decades.

I pushed past these tears of abandonment allowing them to turn into tears of joy for the little one now growing inside me.

Six months.

During his prayer, Zechariah had an unexpected vision when burning incense as part of the temple offering. The angel had announced the pregnancy, but it was hard to accept. I recall my husband's doubt-filled words: "How can I be sure this will happen? I'm an old man now, and my wife is also well along in years." The cynicism must have stung as though we didn't want the promises.

The angel had replied, "I am Gabriel! I stand in the very presence of G-d. It was He who sent me to bring you this good news! But now, since you didn't believe what I said, you will be silent and unable to speak until the child is born. For my words will certainly be fulfilled at the proper time."

A smile crept across my face, and I rested in the all-providing nature of the Lord whom we have served. This was not going to be an ordinary child, he was never to touch wine or alcohol, and he would be filled with the Holy Spirit even from birth.

The angel named him John, but who was this going to be? He wasn't to take on the name of his father Zechariah, was this because of his unbelief? Even now he was unable to talk, and when he wanted anything he motioned to me for it.

The silence was somewhat enjoyable.

Joy bubbled up inside me and my heaviness lifted.

He would be a child of wisdom.

Knock, knock, knock.

A teenage girl's voice rang out from the front door, breaking the silence. It was Mary, my niece.

Mary entered the house and greeted Elizabeth with a sincere "Hello?!"
At the sound of her greeting, the child within me leaped for joy!

But why?
Why the visit to see us at this time?

"My dear Mary, I'm so glad to see you. It's been such a long time. I heard that you were betrothed, and have moved back to Nazareth."

Her face smiled graciously at me with girly laughter, her eyes inspecting me inside and out.

"Yes, aunty, I needed to return to my parents prior to marrying Joseph. The priests urged that I leave to spend time with family in order to prepare for married life."

There was a casual silence between us as we waited for the other to speak.

"Aunty," she paused, waiting for permission to proceed. I was expecting an explanation for her sudden appearance at our home.

"A few days ago I had an encounter with an angel, who said that you were pregnant. I was

elated, and couldn't doubt the angels word when
he told me the rest of the message."

The rest of the message? I was edging for the rest
of the story to come to light. "What else did the
angel say?" I queried.

"He called himself the angel Gabriel — you
know, the one that our prophet Daniel wrote
about in his prophecies."

I knew him well, having studied the law and the
prophets with my husband for many years. Gabriel
had given Daniel the explanation of many vivid
disturbing dreams of future events, for "the very
end of time". Any message that Gabriel would
bring was expected to be handled delicately, as
there could be long term consequences.

Mary announced modestly, "During his visit,
Gabriel said that I was favoured above all women.
He said that I would conceive and give birth to a
son, and to name him Jesus."

Looking intently at me, she waited for me to
affirm her story. I could see that she desperately
needed to share with someone, as her Nazarethan
family might not necessarily have believed her.
"Mary, I believe you. Pease keep going."

"Thank you, aunty. The angel continued, 'Your son will be very great. He will be called the Son of the Most High. The Lord G-d will give him the throne of his ancestor David. And he will reign over Israel forever; his Kingdom will never end.'" Mary recalled the message word by word, as if the angel himself was speaking through her. I could not help but listen with glee as she shared.

She was caught off guard by my steadfast gaze as I became fixated on her words. Her face resonated such peace and tranquillity that I knew this story was not one she had made up. And it echoed my current circumstances with the miraculous conception of this babe within me.

A holy silence enveloped us, our eyes joined in a state of grace-filled understanding upon this shared moment in time. Our hearts beat together, synchronised with what was unfolding before us. And then a flame burned within me, illuminating my mind as to what was happening with us.

"Mary. Mary!"

My exclamation broke the divine silence.

"G-d has not forgotten us, his people."

Quizzically, Mary expected further explanation at my sudden realisation.

"Just before you arrived, I had been grieving through my life story where people had labelled me 'barren' for many years. That hurt badly and I have been ashamed to go out, and instead wanted to hide from the probing looks from others."

I needed a breath to collect my thoughts again as this stung me on the inside once more.

"Indeed, I had felt forgotten, but this turned to joy six months ago when the angel Gabriel appeared to my husband in a vision in the temple."

Mary straightened up, connecting the same angel that appeared to her a few days ago with the temple visit. This was not some random spiritual occurrence, G-d was on the move!

"When he received the vision, he did not immediately accept what was being said, and instead doubted the word that was given. That is why he is mute now — due to his unbelief."

Mary could see the pattern now, and wanted to share more, so I motioned for her to speak.

"Elizabeth, I asked the angel how I would become pregnant, as I was still a virgin. Not that I doubted his words; I just didn't understand how G-d would do this without a man."

I knew exactly what she meant — after all, the baby inside me came through my dead body, much like Abraham and Sarah's child of promise was born. How was she to become pregnant without her husband, and while she is still a child? Mary had not quite entered her youth, having been sent from the temple to spend time with her family before the marriage was to be performed.

Mary continued. "Then I responded to the angel, saying, 'I am the Lord's servant. May everything you have said about me come true.' Which is why I needed to come and visit you."

"Just before he left, Gabriel touched my shoulder and I felt a beautiful holy peace descend on me. It was so tranquil that it felt as though I had entered heaven itself, with no cares in this world to hold me back. At that point I realised the angel was delivering the word of the Lord, fulfilling the message. I think I'm pregnant!"

I could only smile at these miraculous events that were unfolding, and we embraced in tears of joy for some time.

"Oh Mary, G-d has blessed you above all women, and your child is blessed. Why am I so honoured, that the mother of my Lord should visit me?

When I heard your greeting, the baby in my womb jumped for joy. You are blessed because you believed that the Lord would do what he said."

Advent 15:

The Righteous Man

This is how Jesus the Messiah was born.

His mother, Mary, was engaged to be married to Joseph.

But before the marriage took place,

while she was still a virgin,

she became pregnant through the power of the Holy Spirit.

Joseph, to whom she was engaged,

was a righteous man

and did not want to disgrace her publicly,

so he decided to break the engagement quietly.

Matthew 1:18–19

~Joseph's Story~

It was a hard decision to make: Should I expose her act of lewdness to the community, or simply break it off quietly?

Her eyes glistened in the cool of the evening, Mary snuggled closely into my side for a quiet embrace. I had been looking forward to her return for some time, as she had left quickly to visit her older cousin Elizabeth soon after our engagement. She had been away for three months, and had returned with the news that she was to be an aunt!

This joyful news came as a surprise as it wasn't an ordinary birth. Elizabeth and Zacheriah had longed for a baby all their life, and having reached a ripe old age together they had conceded that this blessing would never come their way; they did not expect to become parents so late in life. Not having a family meant more than simply not being able to pass on their family name to a child, but also that they were often the subject of public ridicule. Some said that Elizabeth's unfruitfulness was a sign that G-d had rejected them.

Now, at the end of their lives, that curse had been broken. They relished their newborn, and named him John — though non-one in their family had been given that name. Mary finished the story and gave me a long, knowing stare, and together we gave thanks for the life of their new-born baby, now being held in their hands.

"Joseph." She was a young lady of few words, always listening and weighing up a situation before sharing what was on her heart. Our eyes penetrated the sequence of time as I waited for her to continue speaking.

"Joseph. I have something else, more important than this, for you." I felt an awkward mixture of fear and anticipation rise within me; she had not approached me in this tone of voice before.

My heart began pounding deep in my chest as she started to share the news; and I, for one, was not expecting this. She got straight to the point.

"Joseph, I'm pregnant."

Pregnant? *Pregnant?*

I was aghast.

The shock from her announcement angered me.
Yes, I was angry in myself!
This humiliation is going to tar my clean image.

Shame rose within me like a coiled snake that
had been hiding in the shadows and had struck
without warning.

My mind turned to a fog. I could not process
what she had just shared. It was emotionally
overwhelming. Mary brought my hand to her belly,
further convincing me that this was not a story that
she was making up. I could feel the swelling on her
youthful skin, her stomach pushing to form the
baby that neither of us were predicting.

"But, but … you're not physically ready yet to
have children!" I stammered.

At our betrothal some six months earlier, we
shared our vows, 'till our earthly days part', which
included that we would honour the sacredness
of our bodies towards each other in front of our
community. Together we knew that we would
keep these vows which were a moral and spiritual

code, as both of us were deeply committed to a life of purity and righteousness. Others expected it of us, just as we expected it of ourselves.

Our engagement had been called by the temple priests, after careful planning and discussions with the girl's parents for some time. Mary, the servant of the Lord in the temple, was approaching the age where girls would become women. Her parents, Joachim and Ann, lived near the Sheep Gate, Bethesda, located close to the temple, and had vowed their daughter as a gift to G-d, as an answer to their prayers.

As a result Mary served in the temple to fulfil her parents dedication of her life to the Lord. It was about a decade when it became apparent that she would not be allowed to stay within the temple courts during the time of her monthly period. As a result the priests needed to find her a godly husband that could care for her in the way of the Lord. Naturally this made her innocently young; that is, a year or two younger than the usual age for marriage. The priests ensured events were arranged to keep the temple as a place of spiritual purity.

The method of finding a suitable husband for Mary was established; the priests required the unmarried men to bring their staff and lay it on the altar. One by one, each young man anticipated that his staff would bud which would be the sign to collect the bride, just as Aaron's staff had budded prophetically many centuries before. However, exhausting those who had come without success, the priests called for any other man in the town to come forward, who might be the one appointed by the Lord to take the temple girl to be his future wife.

I was not expecting the appointment. As an older man, my wife had already passed away, I had brought up two sons and now lived as a widower for some time. "Joseph, come forward." The calling seemed somewhat out of place, as my time for marriage and raising a family had already come and gone. Reluctantly, I placed my staff on the altar, and to the astonishment of all, it budded! What did this mean?

A circle formed around me, while a small cheer and hand claps rose from the crowd. The eyes of the priests focused on me, the one who was going to be responsible for raising their girl; the 'unsuccessful' young men could only look at my feet, hiding their disappointment at not succeeding to win a wife at this time.

The seriousness of the situation that had just unfolded gripped me: this girl, not quite at puberty, who had been in charge of altar duties, was to be betrothed to myself, an older man. The betrothal was not something that was pressed against her will — it would only proceed if her parents were to agree to the proposal. On my part, I was required to set aside a dowry, and gain consent for the marriage to take place. The day of our betrothal would include the papers that included the terms and conditions of our waiting period, including what would happen if I were to call off the marriage for any reason. To annul the contract, I would need to initiate a religious divorce which would expose my wife to public humiliation and disgrace. This is something I vowed never to do.

The *erusin* period, the time in waiting, gave the bride time for personal preparation, to make wedding garments, and to get ready for married life; and it gave me time to prepare a place where we could establish ourselves. It made sense that we would raise a family in the community where I had been living and working: Nazareth, of Galilee.

I was already established, so upon our betrothal Mary accompanied me back to our village to live with my relatives and friends. Our community was located in the hills of Nazareth, a day's walk south-west from the sea of Galilee, with Mt

Tabor visible in the east. She was not to stay with me, but with my younger brother Clopas, whose house was nearby, during this betrothal period.

The timing of the wedding day was normally organised by the father of the groom. However as my father had passed away the matrimonial ceremony was to be set up by the temple priests in Jerusalem. Usually, like my first marriage, at the time set by my father, on a day that the bride did not know, the groom would be instructed to collect the bride for the celebration. However this time the priests were to provide direction for the timing of the wedding, and I would meet with them again when the 12 months of our betrothal was getting close.

The bride would need to be in a state of continual readiness: bags packed, well-dressed clothes to represent signs of purity with no stains or spots or blemishes, and the wedding dress ready to be slipped on when the call was made. She could be waiting in anticipation for days or sometimes weeks, not knowing the day or hour that the ceremony would take place.

But now, the dream of a normal married life has just been shattered, and the fear of public disgrace hurt my chest and sent my mind dizzying. Only six months into our betrothal, and she is *pregnant*.

PREGNANT!

My head spun, and I felt physically sick. Breathing deeply, I buckled towards the ground to take in breath.

PREGNANT!

Nothing made sense.

Why would she do this?

Mary herself was raised to obey the Law, being under the watchful eye of the temple priests, and trained for a life of service. And when asked to perform her duties she would often say, "I am the servant of the Lord," with a heart of gratitude, to fulfil her tasks.

How could someone so innocent and pure, with high expectations on her, become involved with someone else?

Wait. Perhaps she was taken advantage of. Who did this to her? What *animal* forced his way onto her while she was away?

The rage in my mind exploded. "AAARGH!" I needed to step away. No wonder she came forward softly with this news. Maybe there was a larger story at play that I needed to hear? Surely there had to be an explanation, a reason why this happened.

"Joseph. Joseph." Her voice was calm and steady, and she held onto her words.

Patiently she waited until I was able to bring myself under control, and then continued with the story. I was sceptical and anxious; her words would have to be tested in time. Only an angel from heaven could convince me whether what she was saying was true.

"Joseph, the reason I went to visit my cousin Elizabeth was that an angel appeared to me. He told me that she was already pregnant, despite her age. Naturally that didn't make sense at the time, though I wanted to believe what the angel had shared and test to see if it was true. This is why I asked your permission to visit her three months ago. When I arrived, I found out that she was already six months pregnant."

"So that's the *real reason* why you wanted to visit her?" I quizzed. I wish she had been more open with me about that, as I had thought that she was going to prepare for our wedding while away.

"Yes." Mary remained quiet for a time, allowing me to dig deeper into my soul and find some level

of truth in her story. The depth of the message
had been kept hidden from me until now, and
I had trusted that our circumstances and vows
would be fully effective to keep all things in order
until our marriage date was set.

"Joseph, there is also more that I must share with
you now." she admitted.

I started to feel sick again. *This is the part where
she admits her failures and asks for my forgiveness,* I
thought. I expected the worst to come out at this
time. My mind raced, looking for an easy solution
to break it off.

"Joseph, when the angel appeared to me, he also
had other news that would impact my life." A
silent pause and a smile crept along her face, not
exactly sure if she knew whether this would come
out the right way, but proceeded with the rest of
the story anyway.

"The angel's name was Gabriel. When he
appeared, his words to me were, 'Greetings,
favoured woman! The Lord is with you!' I was
confused and disturbed at the vision, but was
eager to hear what he had to say."

Mary was not sure how the next bit would be
received, but repeated it word for word, just as it

had been spoken to her. "The angel continued, 'Don't be afraid, Mary,' he said, 'for you have found favour with G-d! You will conceive and give birth to a son, and you will name him Jesus.'"

There it is, *the full confession*. Mary was told by *an angel* that she was going to have a baby. She was even given the name of the baby, and its gender! Was this a carefully planned story to convince me that this baby was appointed by G-d? Was I starting to hear the truth for the first time?

I was hesitant, still not quite sure about what to make of this.

Mary continued. "I asked the angel, 'How can this be, since I am a virgin?' G-d knows that it takes two to bring forth a baby, and we were only betrothed, not married."

Yes, good question. *How were you going to bring forth a baby without our union being blessed?*

"The angel responded to me saying, 'The Holy Spirit will come upon you, and the power of the Most High will overshadow you. So the baby to be born will be holy, and he will be called the Son of G-d.'"

At this, I was still not convinced whether the apparition had come from heaven or if the story was a complete fabrication of events. In my mind, it wasn't the sort of thing a holy G-d *would allow* upon two people who had committed themselves to each other.

"Joseph, the angel wanted to provide me with me convincing proof that what was about to happen was a word sent from G-d. So he gave me one more word, saying, 'What's more, your relative Elizabeth has become pregnant in her old age! People used to say she was barren, but she has conceived a son and is now in her sixth month. For the word of G-d will never fail.' That is why I hurried off to see her. All the words that the angel spoke have come true. And now, so is the case with this baby within me."

Her words seemed clearer, though my mind was not bringing it all together. I could barely handle the gravity of what was unfolding, given our standing in society and among our friends, with respect to the commitments we had made each other.

I asked, "Well, what did you tell the angel? How did you respond?"

Mary looked up, although it had taken all her energy to bring this message to me. Fearing how I might react, she concluded, saying, "I told the angel, 'I am the servant of the Lord. May everything you have said about me come true.' And then he left me."

It would take some time for me to work through all this. If what she was saying was true, then we would have a lot of explaining to do. Everyone in our community would soon realise that she was pregnant during our betrothal, and we would be judged for our actions.

If I didn't divorce her then it would be assumed that I was the father, and I would be ridiculed with disdain and public disgrace. But if I were to break off the marriage, then she would become the scorn of the community and the centre of public disgrace.

Neither of us would be seen in a positive light or received warmly in our community.

In any case, Mary would have to raise the child, who would live with the scorn of being born to an unwed mother, whether he liked it or not. By default, our humiliating situation would become his own, and he would be scorned, despised and rejected.

This was an impossible situation that wasn't about to clear itself overnight.

Why do I feel so torn with no way out?

Can I really believe Mary's message?

And who is this child going to become?

Advent 16:

The Innkeeper

And while they were there,

the time came for her baby to be born.

She gave birth to her firstborn son.

She wrapped him snugly in strips of cloth

and laid him in a manger,

because there was no lodging available for them.

Luke 2:6–7

⁓*The Innkeeper's Story*⁓

I felt a wave of regret the moment I said it.

"I'm sorry son, there is, unfortunately, no spare rooms that I can offer you for the night. You will need to find other accommodation."

Having grown up in our little village, I had known Joseph for many years as part of our community. I had heard that his wife had died a while back so when he turned up under these circumstances it came as quite a shock.

The village was bustling with people, most had travelled long distances to make it back home to be with family whom they had not seen for a long time. It was early afternoon, the markets were starting to run low on food due to the influx of more-than-welcome guests, an air of frenzied excitement was settling on the place.

Joseph looked around, speechless that he was not able to find a room. Guests needed to move through the front door, which made him step aside and peer out onto the streets to think through things further.

The census would commence at the start of the new year, and once completed the families would travel back to their usual place of residence. This headcount served as an important indicator to establish the next decade of Roman rule, so the numbers needed to be right.

"Joseph, I'm sorry that there is no place to lay your head tonight, but I may have a suggestion for you to follow up."

He kept staring into the distance, scanning the streets for a sign to indicate that a temporary room might be available. After a while, he turned to look at me again, waiting for what I was to offer.

"I know you have many relatives and friends here in Bethlehem, but any space for you and your wife might have had would be already gone. If it was just you alone then I'm sure that someone would take you in, but since she is on the verge of giving birth, as you say, then this would be a large interruption to the household overnight."

He could see that this was not just going to be 'an inconvenience' for a family, but the fact that the rumours also appeared true — that they weren't quite married — and *yet she is full term*, ready to give birth at any moment. The snide comments and ridicule from distant family members was something that they wanted to avoid. The Jewish community persecuted those who practised sexual immorality, and in this case it appeared to be a blatant act of hypocrisy where the *temple girl* and *the man of righteousness* had demonstrated impropriety.

Forever this child would be labelled as *the bastard son* and the family would never find acceptance wherever they lived. Joseph would be publicly shamed and made to feel uncomfortable in every setting where people had heard the story. And the child would grow up as an outcast, picked on and rejected from living a normal life — knowing only sadness and sorrow. They would call him 'the son of the carpenter', but that would only be a tongue-in-cheek reference to this unforgiveable situation.

I knew that having no room to offer them would make things even more difficult, but could I be seen to be opening my home and business to them when the opinions of others counted so much? I didn't need to be involved in this dispute, or to drag down our family name by showing sympathy or support to the couple. They needed to work this out themselves with minimal involvement from me.

And yet, I wanted to help them — Joseph was kind of family to me, and it sounded like the situation was becoming desperate. I proposed an alternative. "What if you can find a place out of town, away from people?"

The thought didn't really make sense to Joseph, but he knew that I was referring to the level of ridicule that was expected to come from people who knew of their story. If they could avoid being the centre of attention and find a small lodging out of town then this may help solve their immediate need. And I knew just the solution, though it wasn't anything near the level of comfort that I could provide in one of my rooms.

"There is a small farm on the edge of town, just down the road here. If you approach them, they may find a place for you to stay."

Joseph knew it quite well — he had spent time on the farm as a child, which belonged to one of his uncles and was now operated by his cousins. They raised sheep, and lambing season was already underway so they would be using the stall to shelter the special lambs.

The predicament seemed partly solved in his head, knowing that this would be perhaps the only short term solution to his current dilemma. "Thank you, my friend. I really appreciate your suggestion. I will go at once and see my cousin to find out about it."

He shuffled off down the road, partly jaunting, to approach his relatives who he hadn't seen for some time.

As the manager of my family run business in this small town, I had done everything that could be reasonably expected of me. Realistically there really wasn't any room available at this time anyway, with the important guests already having taken what was available ahead of time. But my heart felt heavy as I closed the door to these people in their time of need.

I couldn't help but think that if the child didn't survive anyway then it would save them a lifetime of ridicule, and they would be better off starting again once they were properly married.

As I turned to enter inside, my eight year old daughter emerged through the door and gave me a loving hug, holding me tightly for a while before looking up into my eyes.

"Who was that, daddy?" she asked.

I hesitated, catching my thoughts before avoiding her question completely.

"Darling, that man grew up here many years ago, and has many family members in the town. He has had to come back like the others to enrol next week, but we couldn't let him stay with us at this time."

Stooping down to her level, I wanted to speak to her face to face and share the deepest thoughts of my heart with her so she would truly understand what was happening.

Quietly, I spoke into the side of her ear. "He is a dangerous man. I'm not sure if I can trust him. I didn't want to bring any trouble on our family while the Roman presence is extensive in town this week."

Her eyes popped slightly, then relaxed, and standing up she let go and ran back inside.

We need to guard ourselves against those who will bring us down.

And in this case I felt I made the right decision.

That baby will never be accepted here.

Advent 17:
The Little Town

But you,

O Bethlehem Ephrathah,

are only a small village among all the people of Judah.

Yet a ruler of Israel,

whose origins are in the distant past,

will come from you on my behalf.

Micah 5:2

⸛The Angel's Story⸛

A heavenly angelic presence hovered over the hilly fields, unseen to the human eye, stationed to watch until the appointed time.

Bethlehem, I have been watching over you for centuries and generations, with promises that have come from the seed of Abraham.

And now it is time to fulfill all that was spoken about you.

Through the generations of Israel, Judah, Perez and Hezron, a man of faith came forth: Caleb. When the twelve spies were sent to the land of Canaan, ten in the group provided a bad report; however Caleb was just one of two who reported faithfully that the land was plentiful and that it could be taken with the strength of the Lord.

Later, Caleb boldly asked for his inheritance, after all his generation had died; his strength had not diminished. Joshua granted him the portion of hill country of Hebron — south-west of Jerusalem — forty-five years after first spying out the land of Canaan. The only thing he was required to do was drive out the three sons of Anak and their families, who were living in the land, before occupying it. And by faith he did so, and settled there.

Bethlehem, you were assigned this territory from the faith of this one man, Caleb.

After the death of his first wife, Caleb moved to the northern part of Hebron and married a lady by the name of Ephrath, and together they had a son named Hur. To honour his wife, Caleb named the town they were living *Caleb-Ephrath*. Later, it was simply referred to as Ephrath, whose name means *fruitful*.

Bethlehem, your birthplace is founded in honour and fruitfulness.

Caleb's son Hur married, who brought forth Salma, and Salma's son was *Bethlehem*. Together they lived at Ephrath. It was one of the smallest clans among the tribe of Judah, in the field of woods at Kiriath-Jearim, in the hill country of Hebron.

Thus when the sons of Caleb took over the region, you became known as Bethlehem-Ephrath.

Bethlehem, although you were the smallest of the clans, you are not insignificant.

Hebron, previously the home of the giant Anakites, also called Kiriath-Arba, was situated south-west of Ephrath, and had long held the settlement of Abraham, Isaac and Jacob. There, Abraham buried Sarah in a cave.

As your ancestor Jacob was travelling to Ephrath, your matriarch Rachel began giving birth with great difficulty. Travelling with them, the mid-wife assisted to bring forth a son, though Rachel lost a lot of blood and was dying quickly. With her final breath Rachel named him Ben-Oni, which means *son of my trouble*. However Jacob renamed him Benjamin, which means *son of my right hand*.

Jacob buried Rachel along the road, just a little distance from you, *Ephrath*, and set up a pillar to mark her tomb.

Bethlehem, out of *trouble* I have birthed *strength*.

Elimelek, an Ephrathite from Bethlehem, during a time of famine moved to the region of Moab, married and had two sons. Tragedy fell upon

the family, and both he and his two sons passed away. His wife Naomi returned to his hometown Bethlehem with her daughter-in-law Ruth.
The whole town was disturbed to see them, exclaiming, "Is this really Naomi?"

A man of renown in the town, Boaz, welcomed them, whereupon took Ruth as his wife to fulfil the role of a kinsman-redeemer to Elimelek. As part of the officiation, the elders of the town and people at the gate blessed them, saying, "May the Lord make the woman who is coming into your home like Rachel and Leah, who together built the family of Israel. May you have standing in Ephrathah and be famous in Bethlehem."

Bethlehem, I have incorporated outsiders into your story and brought you honour from ashes.

Boaz and Ruth had a son whom they named Obed.
The son of Obed was Jesse, an Ephrathite, who had eight sons.
Three of Jesse's sons had followed King Saul to war against the Philistines.
As David was the youngest, he tended his father's sheep at Bethlehem.
The prophet Samuel was sent to anoint one of the sons of Jesse at Bethlehem. After much

investigation, he found David. David was called to be king of Israel after the demise of King Saul.

Bethlehem, I have appointed you to bring forth a ruler.

During the time of King Saul's reign, the priests of Israel did not consult the ark of the covenant. It had been lost in the woods, in the region of Kiriath-Jearim, also known as the field of Jaar.

King David made a vow to the Mighty One of Jacob and prayed for the return of the ark, and the Lord replied with an irrevocable oath, saying:

> "One of your own descendants
>   I will place on your throne.
> If your sons keep my covenant and the statutes
>   I teach them, then their sons will sit
>   on your throne for ever and ever.
> Here I will make a horn grow for David
>   and set up a lamp for my Anointed One.
> I will clothe his enemies with shame,
>   but his head will be adorned
>   with a radiant crown."

Bethlehem, I will raise the horn of my strength in you.

Is it no small wonder that the prophet Micah proclaimed about you:

"But you, Bethlehem Ephrathah,
though you are small among the clans of Judah,
out of you will come for me
one who will be ruler over Israel,
whose origins are from of old,
from ancient times."

And tonight, after centuries of waiting, *Bethlehem*, your time has arrived.

Tonight, I have been appointed to announce the fulfillment of these promises, the bringing forth of the ruler!

There were shepherds living out in the fields nearby, keeping watch over their flocks at night.

A trumpet sounded throughout the heavens, and it seemed that all creatures in heaven and earth paused and turned, waiting for the message.

It was time!

My appearance broke the stillness of the night sky, and the glory of the Lord shone around the shepherds. They were terrified to see me, and hid their faces from the shiny brilliance.

"Do not be afraid.
I bring you good news that will cause
    great joy for all the people.

> Today in the town of David a Saviour
>> has been born to you;
>> he is the Messiah, the Lord.
> This will be a sign to you:
>> You will find a baby wrapped in cloths
>> and lying in a manger."

Suddenly a great company of heavenly host appeared alongside me, praising.

> "Glory to G-d in the highest heaven,
>> and on earth peace to those
>> on whom his favour rests."

And just as suddenly as they had appeared, the manifest angels retreated to heaven.

Trembling with awe and excitement, the shepherds said to one another, "Let's go to Bethlehem and see this thing that has happened, which the Lord has told us about."

Bethlehem, your time has come.

The king has arrived!

Advent 18:
The Stall

And you will recognise him by this sign:
You will find a baby wrapped snugly in strips of cloth,
lying in a manger.

Luke 2:12

⌒*The Mother's Story*⌒

The fresh spring air cusped against my face, and although winter was officially over our journey wasn't. We had travelled the distance from Nazareth to Bethlehem over the last six days, with Joseph leading my donkey all the way until we reached his hometown. This was not a trivial journey, as I was heavily pregnant and we could not afford to slow down until we arrived.

We had planned to arrive before the Sabbath, giving us six days to travel and which also meant that we could keep the requirements of the Law. Today was the last day of our travels, and we needed to arrive before sundown so as to avoid travelling on the Sabbath. And this was not an ordinary Sabbath, we would be welcoming the start of the new year, Nisan 1, once the sun had fallen beyond the horizon.

These circumstances made our journey even
more extraordinary. I was dreaming with cheerful
expectation, upon our arrival, that it would be
refreshing to put my feet up, rest my back from
the long journey and take a hot bath at the local
inn to sooth my body.

Our trip was not something we had planned while
I was in this state, and it would have been better
for me to stay in Nazareth with family instead of
risking injury along the way. However an edict
came from the Roman governor Quirinius for
the family groups to be counted according to
their ancestral divisions, along with their assets, to
determine the rate of taxes that should be applied.

This made the little town of Bethlehem heavy
laden with out-of-towners who were obligated
to be present for the census. As Joseph was
of the lineage of King David, those who were
well respected or well-known were able to find
accommodation, while the rest found lodging
where-ever they could.

It was no surprise then that there was no lodging
available in the inn, as the little village was not
used to such a great influx of people all at once.
My dreams of relaxing in a hot tub vanished
like a mist and my husband-to-be set about

finding a suitable resting place with his relatives and extended family who resided in the town. Meanwhile I sat in the village square with the donkey until he returned to collect me.

From the first day of spring, the birthing of the lambs provided renewed life into the village. It was three weeks since they started to drop, and I felt that my baby was to come anytime during this lambing season too. Indeed the pain in my lower back was starting to hurt. Was this simply from riding the colt to get here? The spasms had grown in intensity, and then start to relax — allowing me to breath normally for a while — and they were increasing today, of all days.

Finally, he returned. He is such a good man with many connections with friends and family. I was sure he would be able to persuade someone to take us in. If this baby was to come tonight, I needed to be in a place with family who could help.

"Mary, I talked with as many relatives as I could find in this short time before sun-down, and it was hard to convince them that we needed a place to stay as they were already taking in others from afar." Joseph's voice sounded partly distressed and melancholic, as though he had failed me. But then he put to me a proposition that needed my careful consideration.

"There is a small stall on the edge of town, outside our village. It belongs to my cousin. They are keeping the special lambs in there with their mothers. He has offered it to us, until we can find another place of rest, if we are willing to accept it."

The disappointment of not being able to take a bath soon vanished with the hope that we would be able to rest from the journey, and have a place that we could call home for the night. It wasn't ideal, but it was the only accommodation on offer at a time when we needed it. I knew we had to accept it, and gave an agreeable nod for Joseph to help me to my feet.

The stall wasn't too far away, about 15 minutes by foot, and we were able to create space towards the back by pushing aside the nursing ewes. This provided us a small amount of roof shelter, keeping us partly protected from the weather.

It was enjoyable to see the newborn lambs standing next to their mothers; we watched as they spent their time together. The smell of the newborn lambs was something that I was not used to, the experience was new and refreshing despite the way I felt from our long travels. Meanwhile we spread out rugs on the soft earth to form our usual night-time layers of bedding and rustled through our bags for the last of our travel food and water.

The tight pangs in my lower back continued to seize me, and as the night grew on Joseph could see that the birth was imminent. Here in the stall there was a heavenly peace that covered the sheep and their lambs, where we could all find our rest. But circumstances seemed to indicate that our rest was likely to be delayed tonight.

A wave of exhaustion mixed with joy, flushed over me, as if the world was about to change forever, the words of the angel Gabriel came to mind. "He will be very great and will be called the Son of the Most High. The Lord G-d will give him the throne of his ancestor David."

"O Lord," I prayed, "will you really be coming tonight?"

Looking around, this place wasn't fit for a king.

This was no traditional birthing suite, and there were no midwives on hand to help with the delivery. At best, the water trough had a source of water for the sheep that used the stall. It wasn't hygienic, and we had limited amounts of fresh clean water on us.

The feed trough, a timber manger that contained the remnants of grain, sat near the entrance. We might be able to use that as a cradle after the birth to lay him in. Due to our travels we brought no clothes for the new-born, and we did not bring much in the way of additional clothing with us. We were ill-prepared for this!

The lambs in this stall were special, dedicated to the Lord for the upcoming ceremony and celebrations. Separated from the rest of the flock, they were to be kept unharmed by wrapping them in cloths and set aside with their mother ewes. This way they could be offered without spot or blemish, an acceptable Passover offering to the Lord — just fourteen days from now. At best, we may need to use these lambing cloths to wrap up our child, there really was no other clothing available to wrap our child that might be of use at this point.

The rest of the flocks in the fields were kept under close watch by shepherds who protected them from lions or bears who sought an easy meal. At least here, in the stall, they were with their mother, kept calm, safe and protected even when no shepherds were around.

The pangs in my lower back increased again, and the joyful sadness of this birth reached into the depths of my heart, knowing that here in this stall, with these sheep, tonight would be born the lamb of G-d, the Saviour of the world — just as the angel had spoken.

Time passed, and my breathing increased to pant through the contractions that were now quite regular.

"Joseph," I called in a soft voice to my weary fiancé, who was resting next to me.

"He's coming!"

Advent 19:

The Shepherds

They hurried to the village and found Mary and Joseph.
And there was the baby, lying in the manger.

After seeing him,
the shepherds told everyone what had happened
and what the angel had said to them about this child.

All who heard the shepherds' story were astonished.

Luke 2:16–18

⁓The Shepherd's Story⁓

I looked up into the deep dark blue of the night
sky where a million stars had been speaking
to us the story of creation. There was always
something to see, and tonight was no exception
as a still holiness descended over flocks under
our care. The night sky occasionally lit up with a
falling star; the identity and formation of various
clusters provided us with plenty of discussion.

Bending over the log pile that we had made
earlier, I poked the fire to provide a small
amount of light and warmth as we tended the
sheep which were resting nearby. The ewes were
keeping an eye on their newborn lambs under
the moonless sky — with the orange lick of
the flames providing occasional visual contact
amongst us and the sheep.

We were in no way attempting to be astronomers, but these vacant evenings together during lambing season gave us plenty of time to postulate the meaning of the signs in the heavens, and to discuss the promises spoken by G-d to our fore-fathers.

We were talking about just how may stars there could be hanging above us, and relating that to the scripture which said:

> *Then the Lord said to him,*
> *"No, your servant will not be your heir, for you will*
> *have a son of your own who will be your heir."*
> *Then the Lord took Abram outside and said to him,*
> *"Look up into the sky and count the stars if you can.*
> *That's how many descendants you will have!"*

"So you see," I reasoned, "all of Israel has come about because of this one promise, and we are all being compared to the number of stars in the universe. There are going to be millions of us coming, to cover the face of the earth!"

My comment ignited a raucous laughter from the crew who found it hard to imagine how this might come about, especially since only a remnant returned from the captivity. We reckoned that it might have been somewhat a joke, given that stronger nations had taken over our land in more recent times. How can G-d keep His promises under these conditions? It would take hundreds or thousands more years for us to repopulate the world enough to fulfil these scriptures.

It was almost time to turn in, though not all of us would sleep; we took it in shifts to stoke the fire and keep watch against the wolves, bears and lions that roamed the Judean hills in search of an easy meal.

The deep blue of the serene night sky gave us a sense of calm, the lambs had stopped bleating, and there were no signs of an attack on our sheep tonight.

It was a silent night, a holy night.

Until …

Suddenly the atmosphere lit with the glow of a thousand lamps and startled us, shaking the men to their knees.

What was this sudden intrusion in such an undignified manner?

From within the intense glow, a being emerged, dazzling bright and shining like lightning. We identified this as an angel, and the radiance of the Lord's glory shone about us. The radiance was hard to look at and the scene was terrifying.

"Men of Judea, don't be afraid!"

The angel's commanding voice communicated to us with dignified authority, and we relaxed a little to allow the intrusion to be less of a shock and more of an invitation to proceed with the message he brought.

The once-terrified faces couldn't help but stare at the tall angelic being suspended above us, hoping they would not be struck down.

What could this messenger want with us?

"I bring you good news that will bring great joy to all people."

My mind raced for answers as the angel spoke; this was not an everyday occurrence for a lowly shepherd. Could this appearance be related to an angelic encounter to a priest in the temple about twelve months ago — just prior to Passover? We had heard about this, and the whole of Israel was nervous with excitement as the Lord has been silent for over 400 years. Was heaven finally breaking through to earth in these appearances?

"The Saviour — yes, the Messiah, the Lord - has been born today in Bethlehem, the city of

David!"

We had been waiting for the promised Messiah, the one whom Moses and the Prophets wrote about, for centuries. All the writings and confirmations from G-d pointed to one who would rescue Israel and fulfil all the promises spoken since the beginning of creation.

If this was the fulfillment of those promises, as the angel had spoken, then we could see G-d's salvation with our own eyes!

"You will recognize him by this sign: You will find a baby wrapped snugly in strips of cloth, lying in a manger."

Now a manger is not a birthing suite for the promised Messiah, is it? The feed troughs are not clean, nor soft. The cloths are not meant for a newborn child, but to wrap the lambs in for the day of their offering to the Lord.

Although the message was clear, we sought for meaning to decipher the code. Or was it as simple as what the angel was saying? *You will recognise him by this sign…*

Suddenly, the armies of heaven broke through and lit the sky above us, filling the hilly landscape with the glory of heaven. They were praising G-d with a heavenly song and singing.

> "Glory to G-d in the highest heaven,
>   and peace on earth to those
>   with whom G-d is pleased."

An amazing blend of vocal variety thronged a chorus sung in unison so beautiful that it felt like both a victory march and a Davidic worship Psalm. We were bathed with the dew of heaven's glory, worship and peace as the angels voices echoed the triumphant announcement through the hillside. Our hearts joined in with the chorus, there was no longer a distinction between those who worshipped in heaven or those on earth — we were all one.

When the angels had returned to heaven, we needed to find this promised child.

"Let's go to Bethlehem! Let's see this thing that has happened, which the Lord has told us about."

And we headed into the little town to find the baby in the manger.

Advent 20:
The Star

"Where is

the newborn

king of the Jews?

We saw his star as it rose,

and we have come to worship him."

Matthew 2:2

⁓The Magi's Story⁓

We are known as the Magi, and are the recognised advisors to the ruling elite for thousands of years. Through us, kings and leaders have sought our wisdom to make decisions and to establish their kingdoms amongst the earth. We are men of renown and stature, though we perform our function quietly, preferring to keep to ourselves until the need arises.

Our body of knowledge captures the mysteries of the heavens and the earth, based around astronomy, medicine and mathematics, which has shaped the course of civilisations. We have preserved the ancient knowledge from the time of creation, and the way civilisation developed after the deluge.

We find purpose and meaning in life from an eternal context, connecting the physical world around us to the elements of time and space through facets of the created order. We seek to understand the mysteries of the universe and allow the elements to speak to us. Through the reading of the signs we can predict and discover significant world events before they are known by kings and leaders. And this is why they seek us out.

After the great flood that destroyed the whole earth, we sought to preserve the knowledge of creation by building a large temple that would reach into the heavens. Our father Ham was sent away into a foreign land in the east, cut off from his brothers for the act that he performed on his father Noah.

In the east, in the land of Shinar, we constructed a large temple that would not only help us overcome any future flood waters, if that were to happen, but was to bring us into contact with the spirits of old that hovered over the surface of the deep abyss at the time of creation. Through our union with them, we would build a super-human race called the Nephilim, who would become heroic warriors on the earth, and would out-live the other survivors of the flood. Using their dark power we would rule over the other sons of

Noah - Shem and Japheth - and take control of the land.

In Egypt, we served as advisors to Pharoah along with his enchanters and magicians. Through our understanding of the stars and planets we developed calendars, and were often consulted to plan agricultural religious festivals. We were called upon to interpret dreams and visions, and provide clarity to Pharoah or others when this occurred.

As highly educated and respected members of society, we were Pharoah's trusted physicians, called upon to diagnose and treat a variety of illnesses through herbal remedies and surgery. And after a funeral we were responsible for mummifying the deceased to ensure that their souls could safely navigate the afterlife.

We were the intermediaries between the gods and the people, responsible for offering food and drink rituals to ensure that the land was cared for and that life would be prosperous. We were called upon for the interpretation of dreams and reading the signs of nature, explaining the mysteries of the unspoken world to whom they were delivered. Indeed, we were messengers of the gods to provide instruction for important decisions to those earthly rulers that were entrusted to our care.

We tapped into the supernatural via means of divination to find things that others could not understand or predict. The use of dark arts, spells and incantations invoked the gods and warded off evil spirits, and we burnt incense and sprinkled water to enact the ritual into practise.

We were the wise men that Pharoah called to demonstrate the power of our dark arts. When Moses and Aaron confronted Pharoah by throwing Aaron's staff onto the ground which turned into a snake, we did the same with our staffs and they all turned into snakes. When Moses called the Nile river to turn into blood, we likewise did the same with our magic arts. When Moses called frogs to rise from the water of Egypt, we did the same by our secret arts.

Our legacies remain alive in the artistic style that we passed onto the Egyptians, the use of vivid primary colours, intricate patterns and a focus on detail. We introduced them to our symbols and patterns, like the ankh and the eye of Horus. From the stars we introduced them to the ruler of the afterlife, Osiris, into the art of Egypt, as well as Sirius, known as the coming glorious prince of peace.

In Persia, our Magi clan was one of six tribes in Media that lived during the time of Darius the king, when the prophet Daniel had been captured as part of the Israelite departure from their land. We undertook priestly duties to perform sacrifices or direct spiritual or supernatural powers, to ensure that the land and life were in balance with the gods.

We operated in influential positions in the courts as dream interpreters and soothsayers. We enjoyed the prominent positions in our society, undertaking our administrative roles with the oversight of kings and leaders.

In time we developed the laws of the Medes and Persians, and through our royal position we ensured that our kings and leaders were appointed once they were able to master the scientific and religious disciplines required by us.

One of our functions was to interpret the dreams of the king of Babylon. King Nebuchadnezzar arose from our clan that attacked and conquered the land of Judah in Israel, bringing back the captives as slaves to his kingdom.

One night King Nebuchadnezzar had a disturbing dream, and demanded that the magi or astrologers be called upon to restate the dream, as well as to interpret it. *This was going beyond the normal reach of our duties.*

"But, O King, your demand is impossible! No one except the gods can tell you your dream, and they do not live here among people." they cried.

One of the Jewish men from the captivity, Daniel, being groomed as one of the court officials, was also called upon to interpret the dream. After asking for additional time, Daniel and his three friends approached the king and presented the vision, and an interpretation to the king. The spirit of the holy gods must have been upon them.

We maintained the teachings of Babylon through our father Zoroaster, who emerged as a student to Daniel; sought to capture the ancient knowledge that was handed down by word of mouth to maintain the consciousness of our fore-fathers. The theological and religious teachings we received were that there was a single god, and a cosmic struggle between good and evil.

These stories from many years past are recorded in our book of prophecies, stored as a testimony for our great and influential work through the ages.

For many years we have been searching for signs in the heavens, observing the position of the stories in the skies, waiting for the next cosmic event to take place. And just *tonight* a new sign has been revealed.

Tonight a constellation appeared that had been predicted long ago, a sequence of events that made one star shine brighter than the rest in that cluster. The star signifies the birth of a ruler, which coincides with an alignment that occurs only once every sixty years - along with attendant planets and conjunctions. Our sages confirm that the formation was not simply a passing comet or other cosmic distraction, but had regal and royal significance.

The formation originated in the celestial region of Virgo, and refers to the long-awaited prophecy of Balaam, that *a star shall come out of Jacob*. As the story in the stars depicts, the prominent subject is the lady Virgo, known as the virgin.

The first constellation of Virgo holds the star Coma, known as *the desired one*; and Virgo's most prominent star is known as Al Zimach (in Arabic) which translates to *the branch*.

From the story in the stars, we must travel to Judah, to seek the newborn infant, known as *the desired one*, or *the branch*.

We believe from these signs that *the virgin* has brought forth the child, and it is our mission to welcome him into the world. We will bring gold, as a tribute to the newborn king on earth; frankincense to honour his deity; and myrrh as an embalming oil to honour his mortality and bring him into the afterlife.

Advent 21:

The Great King

King Herod was deeply disturbed

when he heard this,

as was everyone in Jerusalem.

He called a meeting of the leading priests

and teachers of religious law and asked,

"Where is the Messiah supposed to be born?"

Matthew 2:3–4

~King Herod's Story~

"They've been away for TWO YEARS!"

My anger boiled at an all-time high.

How dare they ignore my commands?

It was early but still dark, my dreams tortured me, awaking me prematurely. I needed to shake this rage out of my head and become more fully awake.

My palace officers had guarded my doorway overnight and cringed, pursing their lips; their faces knew that this was not going to end well for those who double-crossed me. Their fingers started twitching while nervously waiting for my next command, standing erect by the door and not daring to face me.

I had been pacing the room since I woke up. That
dream had angered me and today was not the
day to throw obstructions my way. The issues of
Rome had also been keeping me awake lately and
the threat of another takeover had never been
resolved.

The situation had been on my mind since the
arrival of the magi, who had come from the
north following a star. Everyone feared and
praised them, as they had a reputation built on
wisdom, experience and insight for handling
celestial events that affected nations across many
centuries. They knew the mapping of the stars
and were able to decipher the signs in the heavens
with clarity and certainty, and had followed a
certain star to Jerusalem, and had appeared before
me searching for a king that was to be born.

Upon their arrival in Jerusalem they had been
enquiring, "Where is the one who has been born
king of the Jews? We saw his star when it rose
and have come to worship him."

That was two years ago, and they never returned.

"OFFICERS, COME!"

The palace officers arrived swiftly and turned
to await further instructions, but my mind was

disturbed with heightened levels of anger from these events.

Many years prior to this I had been appointed *king of the Jews* by the Roman Senate. Having captured Jerusalem some 30 years earlier, I assumed the role as king over the territory of Judea and had sent the former king Antigonus off to Rome for execution. The enemies of Rome should be executed, and I was not to have anyone question my authority in this regard.

I set about establishing the Roman empire under my jurisdiction. After completing several large scale building projects I was honoured with the title "Herod the Great", establishing the harbour at Caesarea as a Roman shipping port and appeasing the Jews with the rebuilding of Solomons Temple. The balance of power between Rome and the Jews was in my hands.

I continued to build using the tariffs that were collected in my kingdom, which established me with position and power, and I was not prepared for an infant to steal my title 'king of the Jews'.

No-one, NO-ONE, was going to take away my throne, or title, be it now or later.

My anger resurfaced and I was faced with only one option: *kill them all.*

"OFFICERS, ROUSE THE TROOPS. TODAY, WE MUST MAINTAIN MY THRONE."

The officers awaited additional instructions, so my directions could be implemented without fault or mistake. On previous occasions they had been summoned to arrest my wife, Mariamne, and later her mother Alexandra, who were then executed. They knew the drill.

I had learned from the magi that this child-king was to be born in the Judean country town of Bethlehem, a town of insignificance in my kingdom. Two years ago, TWO YEARS, I had instructed these so-called wise men, saying, "Go and search carefully for the child. As soon as you find him, report to me, so that I too may go and worship him."

If they had feared me they would have known that I was not one to be double-crossed.

But it's been TWO YEARS and they have not returned. Surely it could not have taken them that long to find the child. Were they completely incompetent? Or did they dare take their lives into their own hands and ignore my command?

My tiredness kicked me into a state of rage.

Clearly they had trespassed against me and planned to side with the Jews.

"TAKE A TROOP EACH, AND GO TO BETHLEHEM — THAT BACKWATER TOWN IN THE HILLS."

I paced the floor as I continued to argue the situation in my head about how to end this futile drama.

They knew the town, it wasn't far from the city and the roads were established, making the travel easy. They would be able to complete this mission today and return by nightfall to report the result. I did not expect any retaliation from the Jews, as I had earned their respect from the rebuilding of the temple, and they owed it to me to be honest in all their workings with Rome.

They owed me the respect of being called their king and *I expected them* to comply with my decisions and actions.

But those damned magi deceived me and turned their backs on my command; they are the ones I should punish in order to demonstrate my proper authority, however they are not in my jurisdiction.

And it seems now they are long gone. So I need to take the matter into my own hands and stomp out the usurping of my throne from the people.

My anger boiled again, mixed with fear — this situation could easily escalate out of control, and then my judicial authority would be questioned by Rome itself.

Turning to my men, I voiced further instructions.

"ENTER EACH HOUSE IN THE TOWN. DO NOT SPARE ANY BOY CHILD UNDER TWO YEARS OF AGE."

The two officers faced each other, their eyes almost dancing at the thought that they could kill without having to engage in combat with any enemy forces. This would be a slaughter, much different to the entertainment that was offered in the colosseum, where we watched captured prisoners fight to their deaths.

From Jewish history, we knew that an infant Moses was hidden in the reeds of the Nile River where the daughter of Pharoah had bathed. This child had grown up to oppose Pharoah and lead a rebellion so that the Jews would leave Egypt and the land would lose the free work of the people. We would in no way want this to be repeated.

This time was to be a surprise attack, and there were to be no boys left alive that were two years old or younger, in line with the timing that the magi made to me earlier. Any male child that was hidden should be discovered and killed.

There were to be no survivors and no compassion — despite the wailing.

This was not a time to spare the innocents.

"USE YOUR SWORDS, AND MAKE SURE NONE SURVIVE. I GIVE YOU MY SEAL."

There, the command was given. It would be accomplished before dark, and I could rest again tonight knowing that my kingdom was not to be overthrown by an infant.

The magi may have got away with this deception, however their king would not survive.

The officers left without saying a word.

I was now confident of keeping my title and throne, and called for food.

Long live the king of the Jews!

Advent 22:
The Glory of Israel

Simeon was there.

He took the child in his arms and praised G-d, saying,

"Sovereign Lord,

now let your servant die in peace,

as you have promised.

I have seen your salvation,

which you have prepared for all people.

He is a light to reveal G-d to the nations,

and he is the glory of your people Israel!"

Luke 2:28–32

⁓Simeon's Story⁓

It was forty days from the birth of Jesus, marking
the need for Mary to bring a pair of pigeons
or doves as a purification offering to the Lord.
Together with Joseph they travelled to Jerusalem,
having spent time with Elizabeth and Zechariah
in the nearby hillside of Judea. This allowed six
month John to play with the new born baby
Jesus at his home, though they were likely too
young to remember. Aside from their lengthy
discussions about the angelic visitations and
other announcements concerning their children,
spending this time together during Passover meant
that Mary and Elizabeth could talk about the
various possible outcomes of the angels words.

It happened that I was now an old man — sorry,
a *very old man* — and have been waiting many

years for the fulfilment of a promise from the Lord before I would be allowed to die.

Many years ago, I was one of many scholars responsible for ensuring that the Hebrew scriptures were correctly translated into the Greek equivalent, rendering each words intended meaning into the Septuagint.

Among the seventy scholars doing the translation works, it was my primary responsibility to translate the book of Isaiah. This was a meticulous task, where every character and stroke from the Hebrew text had to be captured correctly to maintain the authenticity of the translation in Greek. Our works were cross-checked multiple times among the scholars to ensure that none of the original meaning was lost, and that no errors were introduced.

While translating one text from the prophet, I insisted that the Hebrew scripture 'The virgin will give birth' should be more correctly translated in Greek to mean 'The young lady will give birth'. To me it made no sense that a virgin could give birth. I argued that the proper narrative would have intended that a young lady of marriageable age would give birth — an alternative interpretation of the Hebrew word 'almah' — and not a virgin.

However the insistence on this interpretation brought me a sharp rebuke through an angelic visitation, who pronounced a decree over my life. I was warned never to change the meaning of the text, but to always seek what the original text meant and ask for spiritual revelation if it was not understood.

"Simeon," the angel said, "since you don't believe the word of the Lord through the prophet Isaiah, the Lord Himself will give you a sign: You will not die until your own eyes have seen this promised salvation."

That was many, many years ago, and I have been waiting for the consummation of Israel ever since. And since that time I have strived to live devout and righteous before the Lord. I knew — based on this promise, or rebuke — that the Messiah would come during my life time, and I waited for the signal that this was to be the case.

As they approached the temple, Mary was carrying the baby Jesus in her arms to dedicate him and perform the purification rites. The Holy Spirit had prompted me to be in the temple this day, and when they arrived I could sense His presence heavy on me, leading me to walk up to the couple.

Mary and Joseph stopped in front of me with an air of expectation. Beckoning to them, I asked that the baby in their care be placed in my arms, while I pronounced a blessing on Him. Gladly, I received the baby Jesus into my arms and looked deep into His eyes. Sweet rays of pure innocence flooded my soul as the baby rested in the comfort in my aged arms.

Turning my head towards heaven, I could now confess that the Lord is faithful to His Word, keeping every pen stroke of the Law and the Prophets in place.

> "Sovereign Lord, now let your servant
> die in peace, as You have promised.
> My eyes have seen Your salvation,
> which You have prepared for all people.
>
> *He is a light to reveal G-d to the Gentiles.*
> *He is the glory of your people Israel!"*

This child's purpose was never in question: He was the fulfillment of the promises to Israel, and to bring the revelation of G-d to those outside the nation.

I handed back the child to His parents, and while doing so the Spirit prompted me to utter yet

another set of prophecies. Calling forward his
mother, I pronounced this blessing:

> "This child is destined to cause many in Israel
>   to fall, and many others to rise.
> He has been sent as a sign from G-d,
>   but many will oppose him.
> As a result, the deepest thoughts of many
>   hearts will be revealed."

At this time the temple priests and scribes
had gathered around and they knew that this
prophecy was spoken against them. They were
taken aback in disbelief and sneered, "How could
this baby have any influence on us? We know his
mother from being raised here in this temple.
And we also know that his father has not taken
ownership of the child — they are not even
married. Even at his circumcision, his father was
not able to name the child."

Their response was not totally unexpected; at
one stage in my life I had also taken offence that
a virgin could be with child. However having
seen the promise fulfilled with my own eyes, I
knew not to oppose the Lord when His prophet
had spoken.

This child was not going to overthrow the Roman
government as Israel's redeemer. He would

instead grow up and live according to the words
of the prophet Isaiah, who wrote:

> "He was despised and rejected —
> a man of sorrows, acquainted with
>   deepest grief.
>
> We turned our backs on him
>   and looked the other way.
> He was despised, and we did not care."

Turning once again towards the young mother,
a deep anguish and grief filled me, as the Spirit
ushered these words to Mary, "And you, lady
of sorrows, will experience a sword to your
soul as well."

It was by no means intended as an insult, and it
grieved my heart to have released those words of
the Spirit. Her fate was to share the grief of her
son, painful as it was likely to be, and that made
me sad.

Knowing that the Lord had fulfilled the promise,
I could now return home to rest in peace.

With those words, the prophecy was complete.

The Light of the world has come!

Advent 23:
The Prophetess

She never left the Temple but stayed there day and night,

worshiping G-d with fasting and prayer.

She came along just as Simeon was talking
with Mary and Joseph,

and she began praising G-d.

She talked about the child to everyone

who had been waiting expectantly
for G-d to rescue Jerusalem.

Luke 2:37b–38

~*Anna's Story*~

It's as though I have been waiting for this moment all of my life.
And now it's here, I can hardly contain my excitement!

The temple has been my home for the last 84 years, and over that time I've seen first-hand the local uprisings and political power struggles to control the precinct and our capital. The nation struggled through a lifetime of anguish while waiting with expectation for the promised Deliverer, the Saviour of Israel. *When will G-d save us from our enemies?*

My father Phanuel was of the line of Asher and was well respected in our Jewish community. Like the fathers of the other young ladies of our time, he consented and blessed my marriage when I was fourteen; however, I did not have children. We had been married only seven years, when my husband was with me no longer. I've lived out my days in the temple ever since, where I was able to spend time fasting and praying, relying on G-d's promises to Abraham, Isaac and Jacob to be fulfilled.

Then today — *today* — the fulfillment of the revelation arrived at the temple. My spirit burst with joy as an intense energy overtook my body, as the parents arrived to dedicate a young baby boy in the temple. They had come with a pair of turtledoves to fulfil the requirement of the purification offering. The law of the Lord says, "If a woman's first child is a boy, he must be dedicated to the Lord." So they offered him to the priests for their blessing while participating in the cleansing ceremony.

The rebuilding of the Second Temple had been decreed centuries ago by Cyrus, King of Persia, which signalled the end of the captivity. It was being rebuilt during the Hasmonean Dynasty and that of Herod. During that time the struggle for power and control over the region was intense. The empire grew outwards from Jerusalem and Judea towards the coast in the west, beyond the Jordan River in the east, and towards the land of Galilee in the north. I watched as the

Hasmoneans held off the Romans for a long time, until Herod took control and enforced Roman rule over us.

The political turmoil for the control of our land meant that we were always subject to foreign rule. We were warned not to resist the leaders that were asserting their power over us, but to be submissive to their authority — no matter who was in control. We had learned from the captivity that it was better to live a quiet life in submission to others, however we held onto the belief that we would be released from the grip of the Roman empire, and that Israel would be re-instated — just as G-d intended in His covenant with Abraham.

During the course of time I saw changes in the kings who ruled the land as well as changes in the temple priesthood. I noticed that while in the position of high priest, they also appointed themselves to be the rulers of Judea, making themselves both king and high priest.

This tradition caught the attention of the Roman governors, and when Herod took power he allocated priests to support his rule. The office of high priest was no longer selected by the priestly tribes of Aaron, as Rome became established with both political and religious rule. It became customary to expect the citizens of Rome to show allegiance formally by declaring, "Caeser is Lord".

But here in the temple, while I was praying this day, was the sign that Israel had searched for. I had known Mary, the baby's mother, for some time. She had left the temple a year ago to become engaged to Joseph who was a priest in the lineage of King David, and had subsequently left for Nazareth to be with Josephs family.

As the temple girl, Mary and I often spent time together as I mentored her through the scriptures and prayer, nursing her as if she was my own child. It was so good to see her again, and when our eyes touched each other once again I could see a radiant expression of quiet hope and solemnity being expressed through her gaze. She emanated a heavenly peace that surpassed any human understanding or effort. We stared with a deep sense of a shared bond towards each other before approaching for an embrace.

Oooooooh. It felt so good to hold her in my arms again, as well as her baby.

Mary, the saint of the Lord.

Some are called to witness the event.

And there are those who are called to carry it out.

Mary was called, and I was the witness.

As I held her baby in my arms it brought me such great delight! The Spirit of G-d moved upon me, my mind filled with confidence about things to come, and was convinced that the religious and political turmoil was coming to an end.

"This is the one we have been waiting for, the promised deliverer of Israel!" My excitement spilled over to all who walked past the couple, who were intrigued with what I was saying.

"G-d has indeed fulfilled His promises, here is the salvation that He has offered!" My temple friends had been anxiously waiting for this day to arrive, and I was able to tell them that the good news of G-ds salvation was here — *right here in my arms.*

As I held this baby close to my chest, I knew that the word of the Lord had been accomplished. I was overcome with a sense of completion, and joyous tears flowed freely down my face.

Looking down at the baby, this was no ordinary child.

The light of the world had arrived.

The promises of G-d were fulfilled.

Advent 24:
The Plan

Yet you brought me safely from my mother's womb
and led me to trust you at my mother's breast.

I was thrust into your arms at my birth.
You have been my G-d from the moment I was born.

Psalm 22:9–10

⁓*The Son's Story*⁓

The boundless expanse of heaven was filled with a mixture of glory, love, grace and truth as the members of the G-d-head came together. Their combined presence was powerful and intense, and the mystery of their co-existence was great.

> The soul contained the mind, will and emotions, and represented Himself as Father G-d.
> The bodily form appeared as a physical manifestation and represented Himself as the Son of G-d.
> The fluid-like connection between the Father and the Son represented Himself as the Spirit of G-d.

In this way the Three were One in purpose, unity and intent. Each part complemented the other to form a unified Being, each with deep respect and love for each other.

Father commenced the meeting; His thoughts and intents had been meticulously planned.

"Son, now is the time to put the plan into effect for all that we have been considering."

From boundless eons of eternity, We had discussed a plan to create a physical realm that would represent the fullest manifestation of Our creativity. This creation would bring Us much pleasure and joy as We would work in it and through it. The heavens and the earth were to be created from the spiritual and physical matter that construed Our substance, and We would fill it with delightful objects. The beings We create would populate both the heavens and the earth to bring Us fulfilment and satisfaction in a created order.

Within Our eternal realm existed a formless void, creative matter with no definition or boundaries, a mixture that exhibited both physical and spiritual substance that was undefined. The material existed as part of Our eternal essence and lacked the clarity that We wanted to see in a created order. There were no rules or boundaries, no distinction between good or bad, simply the presence of objects that co-existed from an eternal perspective.

On this formless mass existed the waters of creation and deep waters of the abyss. Darkness covered the abyss and the Spirit of G-d hovered over the waters of creation. Enmity existed between the darkness and the Spirit that required a long-term solution, they could in no way co-exist like this forever. The plan for creation was essential to remove the darkness so as to create a kingdom of light.

Father continued. "First, We will separate the light from the darkness. Light cannot live with darkness, and the darkness cannot overcome the light. So We will speak the word and this will be the first day of creation." This would be the beginning of the created order.

"Son, You are the light of all creation. Everything in heaven and earth will be created through You, and for You. Things that are seen, as well as unseen. You, Son, will have supremacy over all creation and hold it all together."

Father's voice was firm, his deep penetrating voice resounded within me as I nodded in agreement. Knowing that this is not something that could be taken lightly, once the plan commenced to abolish the darkness the following steps would need to be carried out in complete obedience without wavering.

Father added further dimension and understanding to this plan.

"When We create the heavens and the earth, and fill it with all kinds of animals and plants, it will require careful tending and management. We will create people to look after the earth and to care for the animals. These earth beings will be made in Our image, with a spirit, soul and body, and will be perfectly connected and integrated with Us."

This connection between Us and them would mean that they would know the mind of Father, be filled with the Spirit and walk in the fullness of peace throughout the earth. We would be joined with the earth beings in a heavenly-earthly bond, and they would reflect Our character.

"All creation will be subject to the authority of people, as Our delegated representatives on the earth. Our joy is that We will commune with them, and they will be children in Our family. Son, they will be your brothers and sisters and will be filled with Our glory, shining as radiant beings on the earth."

My chest filled with delight as the details unfolded, knowing that the plan was going to create relationships with those who we would call Our own. Pure satisfaction and joy bubbled up inside Me.

With a sense of sadness, Father went on to explain how the eternal plan would extinguish the darkness, but would not be without cost.

"Son, the creation will be subject to the influence and effect of the darkness. Although everything We create will be good, the darkness will rise up to destroy it. Some of Our angelic beings will leave their heavenly positions and embrace the darkness, and will rise up to steal, kill and destroy what We create."

Father paused, knowing that this was not the fullest extent of the rebellion against the Creator.

"The humans will also turn against Us, following the lies and deception of fallen angels. They will hand their keys of authority over to the deceiver, and will cut themselves off from Our glory. Ultimately, their spirit, soul and body will be disconnected from the fullness of Our relationship. Indeed, they will cut themselves off from Our family and Our glory will no longer reside in them."

My eyes filled with the pain of sadness. For a moment it looked as though there was no point in carrying out the plan. Why should we put into motion a plan that would ultimately cause Our creation to turn and rebel against Us?

"Son, there is one necessary step that is needed to put an end to the darkness." Father hesitated, and I knew that this is where the cost formed part of the plan. "It can only be accomplished if you relinquish your position here with Us and step into creation itself. You must become one of them."

I listened intently to Fathers words, knowing that by stepping into creation I would have to give up My divine position and equality with Father and Spirit to take on human form. In this sense G-d would be represented on earth and people would recognise the One who created them.

"The darkness will not like Your presence in the realm of their authority, and they will seek to destroy You and cut You off from creation. They will think that they have won a major victory over the Light, but this is where Our true victory will reign. To accomplish the plan, You will need to lay down your earthly body and be subject to death."

The mechanics of how the plan would operate grew more and more complete as I listened to Fathers explanation.

The creation would be meaningless unless the plan accomplished the fulfillment of the kingdom of Light and the extinguishing of the kingdom of Darkness. To do this, I would need to relinquish Myself from this elevated heavenly position — where all creation in heaven and earth is subject to Me — and take the form of a servant, or a slave, that would be subject to death at human hands.

"Your death will accomplish all that We have desired for the human race, to restore the fullness of the relationship that We will create in the beginning with people, and to take back the authority from the deceiver. But it will not end there. My Spirit will bring You back to life in physical form, and You will never have to face death again. And I will position You with the Name above all names, and elevate You to the place of highest honour. All creation in heaven, on earth and under the earth will bow their knee to You."

This sacrifice would demonstrate the long-bearing nature of Father's character, His patience and kindness towards people, and restore that which would be stolen from them by the deceiver.

After consideration, Father's approach was the only right way that could destroy the darkness. The creation would be used to set the plan in motion, and would require My intimate involvement. I would need to step into it and become human.

"Father, what is required for me to become one of them?" I asked. Although I sensed that I knew the answer already, I wanted to hear it from Him directly.

"My Son, my dear and precious Son, you will need an earthly mother and father to raise you as a child, just like any normal human has to do. So at the right time, My Spirit will bring You into the body of a young lady who will be Your mother. She will care for You and raise You, knowing that she is partaking of G-ds plan of redemption for the world."

I looked knowingly at Father, feeling the warmth of His Spirit filling Me with confidence that this plan would suffice. It would reconcile all things in heaven and earth, making peace once again with Himself and extinguish the darkness once for all.

"Father, I agree with Your plan, and am delighted that this will work. I will step into creation as You have asked."

Father's pleasing smile penetrated My being, as We agreed these details of the plan.

"There is just one question that will be raised by the humans: What name would You like Me to be known by?"

The answer came immediately, and resonated within Me when Father spoke it.

There really was no other name that captured the level of authority, humility, sacrifice and purpose that could carry out the plan.

We all agreed.

"Jesus."

Concluding Thoughts

I would like to thank you for journeying together
with me in *The Advent* through 24 days of
reflection and contemplation for the birth of Jesus.

On each day we have taken a 'behind the scenes'
look at how events might have transpired for
that person or group of people. We won't know
for sure if the storyline correctly captures the
complete set of events, as the written records
do not include the full depth of history, but I
hope that in no way has it been misleading or a
misrepresentation of the written Word. In some
cases, I've used poetic licence to help us engage
more intimately and I pray that you grant me the
grace to express my opinions and thoughts in
this way.

My aim has been to place you on location into the
timeline for the prophesied birth of Jesus, and

if I've achieved that then my mission has been accomplished. My intent is that you take the time to reflect over each of these promises, taking it a day at a time, rather than to speed-read through the book in one sitting, just like an Advent calendar.

My prayer is that this book moves you closer to Jesus by putting together the promises of God in a logical and concise manner that is easily absorbed.

You may find points of interest or debate in a re-interpretation of the historical accounts, challenging what you may have been taught or learnt. By including a lot of the back-story events we can gain a picture of what might have motivated someone to act the way they did. There is likely to be a much larger story than what I've been able to capture in these few short pages, but I hope it is enough to stimulate further discussion and personal research so that we can grow into a broader sense of understanding of the life of Jesus.

May our lives demonstrate the life-giving work of The Advent by helping us to embrace the promises of God found in Jesus Christ. And may the Holy Spirit grant us fullness of the Presence of God so that we can live powerful lives for Christ.

Brother Brad Smith

~About the Author~

Brother Brad Smith is a Brisbane-born Aussie and grew up in a variety of church denominations in both the city and rural contexts. He has been working with OMF for many years on short term mission trips to Japan. He is married and has two adult children.

Brother Brad has a passion to express the message of the gospel in simple terms and holds a Diploma of Theology from Harvest Bible College, Australia. Brother Brad enjoys writing about theological topics, explaining Biblical subjects in simple terms.

www.brotherbrad.com

Other Books by
~Brother Brad Smith~

In *Via Crucis Via Lucis*, Brother Brad Smith retells the Easter story in a 28-day devotional that carries us through the 14 Stations of the Cross and the 14 Stations of the Light.

Use each chapter of the Via Crucis to enter into a time of reflection, repentance and spiritual growth during the season of Lent.

Challenge your spiritual growth in the chapters of the Via Lucis through purification and renewal during the 40 days after the Resurrection and the 10 days after the Ascension.

Reflect on the readings to participate in discussions between Jesus and the disciples of the first century events during the birth of the Church.

Step into the most powerful moments of history and become part of the storyline.

Available online in ebook or paperback version from **www.brotherbrad.com**

She is highly praised and respected as the mother of Jesus Christ. But who would have known the level of grief that she was to go through when she accepted the calling from the angel Gabriel?

Traditionally identified as Mariam in scripture and translated simply as Mary, she is known by many other names by her devotees, such as the Virgin Mary, the Blessed Mother, Madonna, Mother of Mercy, God-bearer (Theotokos), The Holy Virgin and many others.

Mariam's Memoirs takes you on a journey through the account of her lifetime in this holy position where she recounts the stories at the end of her life so that they can be passed down to future generations. She is considered to be a primary source for the compilation of the gospels in the New Testament.

The prophecy of Simeon in the temple was a declaration of pain that accompanied her throughout her lifetime: *and a sword will pierce your very soul.* As her stories reveal, see how the sword affected her life and calling in ways that we would not have known.

Available online in ebook or paperback version from **www.brotherbrad.com**

9 780645 848137